FORBIDDEN ICE PRINCE

HAVEN ACADEMY: BOOK 1
ARIEL RENNER

CONTENTS

CHAPTER ONE

Walking through the labyrinthine corridor, stalking footsteps echoed behind me. It was only the second week of my first quarter at Huttleston College, but I couldn't help but think that I should have picked a different school. I mean, this one must have been pretty crappy to accept this *entire* group of mean girls. They were the same as they had been in middle school, and they never had been the brightest.

I chanced a peek over my shoulder, and a lock of my wavy red hair fell from behind my ear and into my eyes as I attempted to get a glimpse. Once I swept my hair away, I could see the three of them right behind me: Megan, Louisa, and Heather.

Usually, I didn't take their crap, but I'd been feeling a bit off all day—hot and a little dizzy, like a fever was brewing. Who wanted to deal with bullies on their birthday, anyway? If they wanted to fight again, then I was going to get thrashed. I felt too sick to defend myself at that moment.

But they were right behind me, and the longer they followed me, the more secluded and less populated the area was going to be. If they were just going to keep following me, it would be better to confront them earlier than later.

So I spun around on my heel and stared them down. "What do you freaking want?!"

My exclamation caught the attention of other passing students. This wasn't high school anymore. If these girls tried to fight me now, campus police would be on their asses faster than they could blink.

They may have been idiots, but they weren't *that* stupid. So when they came up to me, I wasn't worried about a sucker punch.

"Oh, we're just here to wish you a happy birthday!" Megan sneered.

"Yeah, happy birthday, Helena!" Heather added, chortling nastily.

I could already feel the heat of rage running through my skin.

"What are you gonna do to celebrate, Helena?" Louisa smirked. "Maybe have a drink? Or two? Get in a car after that for a quick drive?"

A wave of grief crashed over me as the horrific memories flashed through my mind, replaying the moment I'd learned that a reckless drunk driver had stolen my parents from me. My grief was quickly replaced with seething anger.

"You bitch!"

My body moved before I could think. I crossed the distance in three quick steps and grabbed Louisa by her hair, pulling her head to me. "I told you. Don't you ever talk about my mom and dad! *Ever!*"

She glared back at me, but she was grinning at the same time. Heather and Megan grabbed me and tried to force me off her, but I kept my grip.

A sharp sting twinged in my right eye, and it immediately began tearing up as it throbbed. But I concentrated on holding onto Louisa, even as the others pulled my hair and hit me.

Her smug smile burned into my retinas. The scalding anger coursing through my veins felt like it could burst into flames.

Then it did.

A blaze of orange fire exploded in my face. I blinked hard. My eyes stung and streamed. I let go.

Louisa screamed. Megan and Heather screamed.

I swept my hands over my watering eyes and saw Louisa's hands flapping around her head—her hair ablaze. Megan and Heather were both screaming as well, and Louisa was just standing there, howling. Heather was scrabbling through her bag as she panicked.

Bystanders were also making noise, some with phones to ears, but it was all quickly becoming white noise to me.

The heat that had plagued me all day was gone. Instead, a deep chill ran through me. Every inch of my body was paralyzed.

Heather pulled out a large water bottle and doused the flames. Louisa clutched her bald bright-pink head, sobbing mightily.

I still couldn't move.

What . . . what happened?

Someone grabbed me around the waist and dragged me to the floor. I yelped. Hit the floor. Once I was flat on my belly, my wrists were yanked behind my back.

I cried out, and as I struggled, the word "police" caught my ear.

What . . . ? Police?

I looked over and saw a campus police officer. I was dragged to my feet again.

Oh . . . oh, no.

"You know," the detective said between sips of his coffee, "half the reason I'm asking you these questions is that I'm genuinely curious about how you did that."

"I told you," I repeated, "I have no idea."

He took another swig from his cup as I looked at the shining handcuffs around my wrists, binding me to the table. This interview had been going on for a long time, but it was also going nowhere fast.

"I want my phone call," I told him. "You have to give me a phone call."

The detective chuckled and shook his head.

"Sorry, but this isn't a movie. You don't just get handed a phone. You get the right to have someone told you're in custody."

"Oh."

"It's a safety thing. Do you have the number of the person you wanna call? I'll tell 'em for you."

The names of everyone I knew scrolled through my head. *Who would care enough to help me?* I wondered.

I shook my head. "Never mind," I murmured. "There's no one."

For the first time, a little sympathy knitted his eyebrows together.

"No one? Really? C'mon, you wanted a call a moment ago, and it's probably a good idea to tell someone."

I shook my head.

"Friends? Your parents?"

I cracked the saddest half-smile. "I'm a little lacking in that area."

"Oh," he responded.

I looked up at him. "You can call a lawyer, though. I want a lawyer."

This time, the detective half-smiled at me as he got up from his chair.

"A lawyer. You got it. Do you need anything else? Glass of water, maybe?"

"Uh, a Red Bull, Doritos, and freedom would be great."

The detective broke out into laughter.

"I'll see what I can do."

With a heavy *clunk,* the detective closed the door. As soon as he was gone, my chest started heaving and my eyes stung. My bottom lip trembled. Tears dripped onto the table between my handcuffed wrists. I fought to keep from audibly sobbing, but I couldn't stop myself from gasping helplessly.

Why is this happening to me?! It's my freaking birthday! Dammit!

A crash shuddered through my body, and my ears popped. My throat, caught halfway in a gasp, didn't let me yelp.

Suddenly, a black hole—at least what I imagined what one would look like—obliterated the corner of the interrogation room. A deep, swirling mass of darkness, blacker than black, bent the light and space around its edges. The wall's painted bricks warped around it like a piece of fabric rippling.

What the hell?

Then, a figure stepped through.

It was a woman in an old-fashioned kind of dress—*Victorian Gothic*, I thought—in deep purple, with black lace trimming the billowing skirts, attached to a corset-looking top with long sleeves, puffed shoulders, and a collar that buttoned up to her throat. I gawked at her black hair done up in a tight bun, white foundation, black eyeshadow, and plum lipstick that stretched in a warm smile.

The woman stepped through the black hole, leaned down, and brushed some imaginary dirt off her skirt.

"Dear, dear!" she sighed. "Well, *that* was an endeavor!"

She then strode right over to me, looking at my handcuffs.

"Tsk!" she tutted.

The woman brought out a single finger and tapped my handcuffs. They snapped open.

"Come along, now!" she instructed. "It takes a lot of magic to keep a portal open in a place like this, you know!"

She then spun on her heel and began walking back toward the black hole. I was still staring at her, dumbstruck by this Mary Poppins lady who'd just broken into a police cell for me.

She paused at the edge of the portal.

"Come along, now! Chop, chop!"

I found my voice. "W-wait! I can't leave!"

The woman frowned.

"Why not?"

I looked around pointedly. "Uh, I'm under arrest? If I leave, I'm gonna be in *so* much trouble!"

The lady just gave a hoity-toity laugh. "Oh, don't worry about that! I'm taking you to the Enchanted Realm. After we've had a little chat, you can be returned to this very second if you choose!"

I paused at that.

"If you truly don't want to come, that's fine, too. I just thought you'd want to know about your powers after the birthday you've had, Helena."

I straightened up when she mentioned my powers. Even more so when she mentioned my birthday—and my name.

I considered my options.

Option A: Go with this mysterious lady through the magical portal to understand my powers—a once-in-a-lifetime opportunity, I was sure.

Option B: Stay here in the police cell, not knowing what the hell just happened, and try to talk my way through the police procedure.

Well, when you put it that way, the choice was obvious.

I stood up and walked toward the black hole. The woman nodded and smiled at me. "Wonderful! Now, remember to hold your breath as we go through!"

She then stepped into the portal and . . . melted into it.

I took a deep breath—then stepped inside.

It felt *horrible*. As if my body was unzipped and thrown around weightlessly. Like I was put in a washing machine. I only realized had weight again as I fell.

I hit the floor on my hands and knees. I was in a grand office with dark red walls, lined with mahogany bookshelves and stuffed to the brim with old books and taxidermy animals. In front of me was a large desk, also dark mahogany with a red leather surface. The woman sat behind the desk, the French windows behind her illuminating everything. She spread her arms wide. "Welcome, Helena! I am Headmaster Moira, and welcome to Haven Academy!"

"What is this place?" I asked, getting to my feet.

"Haven Academy was created over two hundred years ago for young Enchanted to learn to harness their powers!" Moira declared proudly.

I crossed the room and sat in the chair opposite her desk.

"Most Enchanted are born in the Enchanted Realm, so they grow up knowing they will eventually have special abilities. It's very unusual for an Enchanted to be born in the Unenchanted Realm, but the moment I felt you use your powers today, you became such a beacon throughout time and space that I couldn't look away!"

While my head reeled, Moira leaned her elbows on the desk, linked her hands, and leaned her chin on them.

"I'd like to offer you a place here, Helena. If you stay here, we have mentors who can guide you in using your fire powers. They can show you how to control it, and you can put them to use somewhere in the Enchanted Realms. You can start a new life."

She gave me a sympathetic smile.

"I know your life has hardly been a picnic, dear girl. So, I offer you this choice. Stay at the academy and learn to control this marvelous gift you have. Or you can return to the police station in which I found you. Your choice."

CHAPTER TWO

I t genuinely took me a second to wrap my head around it all enough to utter a word.

"S-so . . . why do I have powers now?" I asked.

"Nearly all Enchanted inherit their powers," Moira answered. "Were your parents Enchanted?"

"Not that I know of," I answered. "They died in a car accident when I was twelve."

Moira smiled compassionately. "I'm sorry to hear that. Having your powers manifest can be a scary thing, even if you know it's going to happen. These abilities we possess are both amazing and terrifying. If we don't know how to control them, we can hurt ourselves and the people around us. That's why Haven Academy exists."

"Right . . ."

Moira's expression turned solemn when she met my eyes. "In all seriousness, Helena, your powers are extremely strong and very dangerous. They can do much worse than what happened today if you don't get them under control.

I know everything must seem overwhelming right now, but I ask that you give us a chance. You'll quickly get used to everything, and you need the training."

I gave a light shrug.

"Sure. You've seen my life, right? There's nothing for me out there, except for a prison sentence, maybe."

"Excellent! That's the spirit!"

Moira pressed a small green gem on her desk, which glowed before she spoke into it. "Please send in Iris."

There was a little sound behind me, and I turned and looked at a set of grand double doors. One of them creaked open. A skinny, pale girl with deep blue hair came in and gave me a meek little smile, wringing her hands in front of her. She wore a school uniform, which comprised a deep plum blazer, a white button-down shirt, a knee-length red plaid skirt, and black loafers. On her blazer was a silver pin of a stylized letter *E*.

"Iris, this is Helena," Moira introduced. "Helena, this is your new roommate, Iris."

"Nice to meet you," Iris said softly.

"You too," I said.

"Your belongings were already set up in your dorm," Moira continued. "Iris will show you around the academy. You'll find your class schedule in your room as well. Classes began on Monday, so you're only a few days behind. I expect you'll get up to speed in no time. Your mentor will expect you tomorrow at 9:00 a.m. sharp."

I had so many questions and so little time and brainpower to comprehend it all.

"Iris, please show Helena to your dorm."

"Yes, Headmaster."

"Okay . . ." I said. "Thank you, Moira."

"Headmaster Moira, since you're a student now," she prompted me delicately.

"Thanks, Headmaster Moira."

The main hall of the academy was a large, impressive spread of white marble stone, with thin gothic windows and red drapes held aside with gold tassels to let the light in. It reminded me of a grand cathedral more than anything else. There was enough room for at least a dozen people to walk, shoulder to shoulder, so when we crossed countless students, we didn't have to bump into anyone.

"So . . . um," Iris stumbled, "here is the library . . . And here is the cafeteria . . . That over there is the Healing Center."

I nodded, glancing inside each room as we went. As we walked, a huge expanse of green came into view through the gothic windows.

"Through there is the gymnasium and field. That's where we all spend most of our time."

"Cool."

"Do . . . you have any more questions?" Iris asked quietly.

As I thought, I felt distant gazes burning into my head. I turned and met the eyes head-on. The gaggle of girls who were looking at me flinched and huddled back within their group. The mean girls back home flashed through my mind.

"Uh, how are the other students?" I asked, wondering if now I had to worry about mean *magical* girls. "Does everyone get along, or is there a group of people I should avoid?"

"Oh," Iris said knowingly. "To be honest, people just . . . stay with themselves for the most part."

"What do you mean by 'stay with themselves'?" I asked.

"Students usually stay with their own guild. Earth with Earth, Fire with Fire, you know? Other than that, people might be friends with those in their dorms. The dorms are mixed-guild."

"What's a guild?" I asked.

Iris had a confused look for a second and then softened. "Oh, yeah. I keep forgetting you're not from our realm. The guilds are based on the powers you have. It's what these pins mean." She pointed to the *E* in her blazer. "I'm in the Earth Guild. You're in the Fire Guild. They're also where we come from. This academy has students from the Earth Kingdom, Fire Kingdom, Storm Kingdom, and Ice Kingdom. That group over there is from the Ice Guild."

I looked over to where she gestured. I didn't know an entire group of people could radiate with cold, their pale skin contrasting starkly against their purple blazers. Several of them even had white or silver-colored hair.

One of them caught my eye. He was tall and broad, with pale skin and snow-white hair. His face was sharp with defined cheekbones and a long face. He looked at me suddenly. His eyes were icy blue, and they burned into me with distinct disdain, freezing me in my tracks.

"Who's that?" I asked Iris, still staring at him.

"That's Fannar. He's one of the top students at the academy."

"Why is he glaring at me like that?" I asked, bristling under his gaze. He was still looking at me. Those polar blue eyes were stabbing right into me.

"Hmm, I don't know." Iris shrugged with little thought. "I mean, well, you *are* Fire."

"So?" I broke his gaze to look at her.

"The Ice Guild and Fire Guild are natural enemies. They tend to not like each other. Don't take it personally." She gave a sympathetic smile.

I frowned. I didn't like the idea of already having enemies just because of the type of powers I had. I looked back at him, and he was still looking at me from the corner of a narrowed eye. But then Fannar looked away from me, disinterestedly.

"Come on," Iris said lightly. "Let's go to our dorm room."

"Okay . . ." I murmured slowly, my gaze still on Fannar.

⸺⸺⸺

The girls' dormitory was just as impressive as the rest of the academy. It reminded me of a classy hotel. The marble hallways were lined with mahogany doors, each one offering a unique glimpse into the lives of the students who lived within. Most were uniquely decorated with bright stickers, strings of lights, motivational quotes, photos, representations of hobbies, and colorful nameplates in fun shapes. A few doors were undecorated, except for two simple metal nameplates. "Two people per room, then?" I asked.

"Yes," Iris replied. "But there's plenty of space in there for two, so don't worry."

We walked three doors down, and she stopped at a completely plain door. No nameplates. No decoration. Nothing.

I looked at her.

"You're . . . minimalist, then?"

"Oh." Iris looked at the door, then blushed delicately. "No, I just didn't want to decorate the door before I had a roommate—just in case they didn't like it." She smiled lightly at me. "You can choose what our door looks like."

I couldn't help but return her smile. "Aw, thanks, Iris! We'll decide it together later, yeah?"

She nodded. "Yeah!"

She then took the handle. "The inside is already furnished, so we don't need to worry about that."

Before I could ask anything else, the door swung open. The room was bigger than it physically should have been from the outside, but at that point, I wasn't surprised.

Each side of the room was the size of a decent bedroom, and all my things, placed where I put them in my university dorm, looked very sparse in comparison. My beloved music box sat on the bedside table. The sides of the cherry-wood box were etched with intricate swirls, and the lid had an artful carving of a simple mountain. There were a few things on the wall as well—just a couple of simple watercolors of mountains. Nowhere I'd ever been but had dreamed about visiting.

The other side of the room was Iris's half. Blue everything—blue peacock bed, fairy lights wrapped around fake blue flowers, and a *lot* of books.

Iris sat on her bed, grinning widely. "I'm so happy that you're such a nice person. When I heard I was getting a roommate this morning, I was worried. I figured you were a Fire Enchanted from your volcano stuff."

"Volcano stuff?" I asked.

"That artwork." She gestured to the wall. "Even your pretty music box."

I chuckled, looking at my things again. "I guess they do look like volcanoes."

"They match your Enchanted mark, so I just assumed."

"What Enchanted mark?" I asked.

Iris pulled down the collar of her shirt and held her hand just under her right collarbone for a few seconds. When she removed her hand, a little green mark appeared. I leaned closer to look at it. It looked like a little outline of a tree, each tiny leaf a neat, delicate swirl.

"Oh, cool!" I exclaimed.

"You should have one, too," Iris said. "It shows up when your powers do. You just need to hold your hand over it to make it appear."

I pulled down my collar in front of the mirror and mimicked what she'd done. Iris was right. A little red outline of a volcano appeared under my collarbone, but there was a light blue snowflake in the middle of it.

Iris leaned forward, and her eyes widened with surprise. "Wait . . . those are the marks of Fire *and* Ice!" She excitedly looked up at me. "You have ice powers, too, Helena!"

"Do I? I only found out about the fire . . . maybe an hour ago."

"Seriously, I've never heard of someone with *two* marks before!" Iris chirped.

"Great, I'm just full of surprises," I quipped sarcastically, but I secretly hid my pride.

I looked at the mirror as my Enchanted mark faded away.

This morning, I'd woken up to a pretty boring future. If I were lucky enough to graduate, I would have an office job that I hated every day and a mountain of debt to chip away at. Now, I was at Haven Academy in the Enchanted Realm. I had no idea what was in store for me, but there was something exciting about having an unknown future. Either way, it would be a magical adventure, right?

CHAPTER THREE

"Helena!"

I groaned.

"Helena, wake up! It's eight-thirty! We have to get breakfast!"

I gave another groan and opened my eyes. My typical mountain (volcano?) painting still faced me, feeling like home. But it hung on white marble walls, and when the light started pouring into the room, Iris drew back the dark red curtains from the gothic windows and fastened them open with a gold rope.

That's right . . . I'm not home, I realized in my daze.

Half of me expected the day before to have been a dream, but I was glad it wasn't. If it was a dream, I would have been waking up in a police cell at that moment.

I slowly creaked up into a sitting position, and a lightweight bundle fell onto my lap.

"Here," Iris said. "This is your training uniform. We have ability training in the gym this morning."

I held up a plum-colored gym shirt and black leggings. "Aren't we a little old for uniforms?"

Iris gave me a sad half-smile and shrugged.

I put the uniform on, and we both stepped out of our room and joined the flood of purple blazers heading toward the cafeteria.

The cafeteria was more like a ballroom with tables as far as the eye could see. But everyone made a beeline to a queue along the side wall.

"Ah!" Iris sighed as we found our place in line. "We got here a bit too late. We really should have been here at eight or even seven this morning."

We had to wait for a worryingly long time, but eventually, we ended up at the front of the line. I was expecting there to be trays full of steaming food, like an all-you-can-eat buffet, but there was nothing there. Just a flat silver hot plate.

Then, from behind the hot plate, a chef's hat appeared, framed on either side by tall red ears. Then, bright yellow snake eyes fixed on me.

"Oh, my God!" I shrieked. "What the hell is that?!"

Iris gave my arm a small slap and spoke louder than a murmur for the first time since I'd met her. "Helena! That's Frankie, our chef gremlin! Don't be so rude to him!"

I paused, and Iris looked sadly at the gremlin. "I'm so sorry, Frankie! She's new . . . and she couldn't see you properly behind there!" She looked at me. "Right?"

I looked at Frankie. The red ears had drooped, and those yellow eyes looked very sad.

"Yeah, sorry. I didn't see you down there."

He still looked very sad, and Iris cut across quickly. "Could I have muesli today, please, Frankie?"

A melancholic, inhuman chitter came from behind the counter, and a pair of three-fingered hands appeared over the top of the hotplate, making elliptical motions. Then, a small ribbon of fog streamed in, swirling together—and a bowl filled with oats, nuts, and fruits and a small jug of milk *popped* into existence.

Then, the eyes looked at me.

"Uh . . . waffles, please?"

Again, the motions happened, then the *pop,* and a steaming pile of three waffles with a pot of butter and a jug of maple syrup on the side manifested.

"Thanks, Frankie. Looks great!" I tried to reassure him.

Frankie just gave another sad warble and looked at the person behind us. Iris and I shared a glance, then we grabbed our breakfasts and shuffled shamefully away.

Okay, this world has gremlins. Got it. I made a mental note to keep my reactions in check in case I came across any other new creatures. I certainly didn't want to offend anyone else on my first day.

As we walked to the gym after breakfast, I took in the impressive gothic architecture of the halls again.

"This place is so weird." I shook my head in amazement. "When I got here yesterday, Headmaster Moira and the building looked so gothic and Victorian, so it felt like I was transported back in time, but you have all the modern stuff I have back at home. Plus, you have a magical chef."

"Well, the academy is old, but the headmaster just likes to dress like that." Iris giggled. "Frankie is special to Haven Academy, too. I heard other campuses have a normal cafeteria staff. Where's the fun in that?"

As we entered the gym, I saw it was separated into several areas. But before I could take it all in, there was a large *crash*.

There was a thundercloud *inside* the gym! It hovered overhead, grumbling away. A girl was standing below it with her arms outstretched. There was a black sooty spot on the mat in front of her, and a boy with bright red hair collapsed onto his back. The burned spot on the mat slowly disappeared, as if nothing had happened.

"How is that possible?" I asked out loud by accident.

"Oh, the mats, our training uniforms, and even the inside of the gym itself are mostly immune to our powers," Iris answered.

A professor dressed in a purple polo shirt bearing the words "Haven Academy" blew a whistle, holding a hand up to the girl summoning the storm in a *stop* motion as he did. The girl lowered her arms, and the cloud dispersed. The professor helped the boy up to his feet.

It's a sparring match, I realized.

It wasn't the only one either—the gym was split into four large sparring areas, and something interesting was happening in each one. One of them had two girls, one with two mini storm clouds hovering over her hands, the other controlling long vines. Another had a boy and girl, each holding their palms forward, with jets of fire meeting in the middle of the mat.

I realized I'd stopped walking and was staring foolishly at the surrounding magic when Iris grabbed my arm and pulled me toward a mat in the far corner.

"Professor Stanton!" Iris called to an older man with golden yellow hair and red eyes, who also wore an academy polo shirt. "We're so sorry for being late! This is Helena."

He gave me a warm grin. "Nice to meet you, Helena."

The warmth in his tone and his smile immediately made me relax a little.

"Yeah," I said. "Sorry I'm late. I didn't think breakfast would take so long."

He broke out into hearty laughter.

"Yeah, that's a real problem. Nothing you can do but get up earlier. Frankie's doing his best! Welcome to the class. We'll get started soon."

"I'll see you after class," Iris said over her shoulder, walking away toward another part of the gym.

A few first-year Fire Guild students gathered around loosely.

"Hey there!" A friendly-looking guy with a mop of blond curly hair greeted me with a beaming smile. "You must be Helena. I'm Jimmy. Go Fire Guild!"

"Thanks, Jimmy," I replied, trying to sound confident, though my palms were sweaty beneath my gloves.

"Helena, right?" A girl with short brown hair and an air of calmness approached me. "I'm Dawn. Welcome to Haven!"

"Nice to meet you, Dawn," I said, exchanging a warm smile with her.

From the corner of my eye, I noticed a tall girl with long, flowing black hair sneer at me.

"So, you're the new Unenchanted Realm girl?" she scoffed, her sharp blue eyes sizing me up with disdain. "Let's see if she can actually handle magic."

"Hey, cut it out, Angela," Jimmy interjected, his voice firm but kind. "She just got here."

"Whatever," Angela huffed, rolling her eyes before walking away.

"Alright, everyone!" Professor Stanton called out, drawing our attention. "Today, we'll be working on controlling the intensity of your flames."

"Remember," he began, addressing the whole class, "controlling your fire is a delicate balance. Too little power, and it's ineffective. Too much, and you risk harming yourself and others."

Professor Stanton demonstrated by effortlessly summoning a small flame, gently flickering in his palm, then focusing his gaze to intensify the fire into a miniature inferno.

"Your turn," he told us.

We started practicing, attempting to mimic his effortless control. The other students around me easily summoned small flames in their hands. My heart raced and my palms felt slick with sweat as I tried to focus my thoughts and channel my energy into creating a spark. I closed my eyes and . . . *nothing*. I tried again and . . . more of nothing.

After several unsuccessful attempts, my cheeks heated up as I imagined the others watching me with amusement when Professor Stanton noticed my struggles.

"Helena, join me over here," he beckoned, and I hurried to comply. "Show me what you can do."

"Ummm," I said hesitantly, "I just learned I had powers yesterday. Don't get your hopes up."

Professor Stanton chuckled. "Don't worry about that. You weren't the first, and you won't be the last. Let's just see what you can do."

"But I don't even know how to start!" I protested worriedly.

"Ah. That's where we are, are we? No problem!" Professor Stanton walked forward. He held his hands out, palms upward. "Give me your hands."

I did. His hands were burning hot.

Then they somehow got hotter. And hotter.

But there was an odd phenomenon. Every time the heat of his hands cranked up another notch, I only felt it for a moment before my own hands adjusted to the heat.

Then, there was a burst of light—both our hands caught fire.

"Whoa!" I gasped.

"Now," Professor Stanton said, taking his hands back, "I've given you a head start, but fire is the power of the passionate. If you want to keep it burning, you need to dig deep and find something that lights your soul up."

"What does that even mean?" I asked, watching my hands as they blazed.

"Well, think about something that you're excited about. Or something that makes you angry. Or something that makes you determined. Try it."

I narrowed my eyes. My first thought was of the bullies, but then I remembered the image of Louisa—her head bleeding and peeling, her screaming—and guilt raced over me. The fire in my hands dimmed.

My next thought was about how people reacted when my parents died. I had never been a good kid, but now that they were gone, teachers and students alike looked at me with both pity and contempt. I never heard it said, but I could see it in their eyes: *Well, she's going off the rails. No doubt about it.*

Some were sympathetic, but I could've sworn some of them wanted to see me fail.

Well, they won't.

The fire in my hand flared higher and higher.

Not only will they not see me fail... I'm going to succeed!

Pulling in a deep breath, the same crawling heat I'd felt the day before crept through my body. The fire in my hands grew at least a foot high.

Professor Stanton clapped his hands. "Excellent, excellent! You're a natural!"

Fueled by my progress, I smirked a little at him and took another deep breath, forcing the energy ricocheting around my body to course down my arms. I turned my hands from cupping the fire to facing the sky.

Fire exploded out of my palms as a cascade of flame crashed into the air like a dragon's breath. Orange blossomed out into the air all around us.

"Wow, Helena! That's amazing!" Dawn cheered, her eyes wide with admiration.

"Seriously impressive!" Jimmy agreed, grinning from ear to ear.

"Thanks, guys," I replied, my cheeks flushing with happiness.

A commotion started around us from students from other classes. Some gasped. Others cheered. The stream of flames still flared in a pillar of fire from my hand. Students and other teachers alike gawked at me, every one of them showing the same expression: eyes wide, jaws hanging open. Even Professor Stanton's red eyes were bulging out of his head. Only two people looked at me with any other expression: Iris, who smiled widely in excitement, and that guy from the other day . . . whatever his name was—the gorgeous ice one. Those chilly eyes were looking at the fire. The last time I'd seen him, he had looked disinterestedly contemptuous. Now he looked *angry*.

Another student leaned over and talked to him, and his intensively bitter eyes looked down at me. He looked like he *hated* me. He looked like he wanted to come forward and take a swing at me at that moment.

I could only glare back. *What is his problem?*

My heart started to race. He exuded a captivating yet infuriating magnetism, scowling at me with those intense, piercing eyes. Despite his toned, statuesque figure, his pale skin and long, white hair gave him an ethereal appearance. He was extremely distracting. I struggled between the urge to slap him across that beautiful face and capture it in a lustful kiss.

He finally broke my gaze, turning around and forcing his way through the crowd that had gathered around me.

Shit, I'm not paying attention to my flame!

Much to my dismay, it quickly grew out of control, flowing up to the gymnasium ceiling, and I didn't know how to stop it.

"Uh, Professor," I said urgently, "some help!"

Professor Stanton quickly stepped in and extinguished the flame with a wave of his hand.

The crowd murmured around me. I bit my lip, feeling embarrassed that I allowed myself to get distracted and lose control, but Professor Stanton began clapping loudly.

"That was amazing! Truly spectacular!" He gave me a playful frown. "Are you *sure* you just discovered your powers yesterday?"

I nodded sheepishly, heat blooming in my cheeks. "Sorry, I almost burned down the gym."

"Ha! Don't worry, Helena." He clapped a hand on my shoulder. "Those are some of the strongest powers I've ever seen from a new student! It'll take time to learn how to control them. But you did great."

"Really?" I replied. "Thanks!" It felt amazing, too.

CHAPTER FOUR

A nother burst of flames erupted from my palm, singeing my eyebrows. Nearby, students jumped back to avoid the unbridled blaze. The heat radiating from the fire left my skin slick with sweat, making it even more difficult to maintain control.

"What the hell?" Angela exclaimed. "You're going to kill all of us!"

"Ignore her," Dawn whispered encouragingly as she concentrated on her own flames. "You can do this."

"Don't forget to breathe," Professor Stanton advised me, his keen eyes noticing my tense posture. "Relax and trust yourself."

I nodded, took a deep breath, and tried again. This time, I managed to coax a medium-sized *and* controlled flame into existence. Its warmth brushed against my face, the crackling sound of burning embers filling my ears.

"Woo-hoo!" Jimmy exclaimed, clapping his hands.

"See?" The professor grinned. "You're getting the hang of it already!"

"Thanks, Professor," I replied gratefully, trying to maintain my focus on the flame as I glanced at Jimmy and Dawn. "And thanks to both of you, too."

"Keep it steady now," Dawn advised, watching me intently. "You don't want to lose all that progress."

Over the days that followed my first training session, I practiced relentlessly. Despite the exhaustion and frustration, I refused to give up, fueled my determination to prove myself. I appreciated the support of the professor and classmates like Dawn and Jimmy. To be completely honest though, the idea that Fannar, the stunning Ice Enchanted, could be watching me from across the gym spurred me to work five times harder.

"See that?" I said triumphantly one afternoon as I managed to extinguish a small fire with precision. "I think I'm finally getting the hang of it!"

"Definitely!" Dawn agreed with a wide smile. "You've improved so much in just a few days!"

"You need to slow it down, Helena," Jimmy added with a wink. "You're making the rest of us look bad!"

"Alright, everyone!" Professor Stanton called out as we gathered around him. "Today, we'll be practicing creating intricate fire patterns. This will test your control and precision with your abilities."

After some instruction, I focused on the small flame burning atop my right palm, willing it to dance and twist into elaborate shapes. To my surprise, the flame complied, spiraling and weaving through the air like a living ribbon of fire, their chaotic energy transforming into a mesmerizing display of light.

"Helena, excellent progress!" Professor Stanton called out. "Remember, your emotions may fuel the fire, but you must learn to channel them properly. Don't let them overpower you or you risk losing control."

Sweat trickling down my brow as I nodded and concentrated on maintaining the delicate balance needed to keep the pattern intact.

"Good, Helena! Keep it up!" Dawn shouted encouragingly from across the gym, her own flames swirling around her like an ethereal ribbon.

"Thanks, Dawn!" I grinned, feeling a surge of pride as my confidence grew.

"Please," Angela scoffed from a few feet away, rolling her eyes. "It's not that great."

"Give it a rest, Angela," Dawn shot back, her protective nature flaring up. "Helena's been working her ass off."

"Whatever," Angela snorted, turning away dismissively.

"Don't let her get to you, Helena," Jimmy reassured me, placing a comforting hand on my shoulder. "You're doing fantastic, and she's just jealous."

Feeling a renewed sense of determination, I resolved to challenge myself even more. I brought forth a ball of fire into both of my palms before painstakingly shaping it into a miniature bird. Then I tossed it up into the air so it appeared to soar into the rafters of the gym.

"Unbelievable," Angela whispered with amazement.

"Beginner's luck," Anna grumbled, glaring at me before attempting the same feat—only to create a clumsy, misshapen blob of fire.

"Keep practicing, Angela," I said, unable to suppress a triumphant grin. "You'll get there, eventually."

Over the course of the next three weeks, my powers grew stronger, as well as my control over them. Under Professor Stanton's guidance, I pushed myself harder than ever before, finding myself in the gym after classes ended.

"Alright, everyone, pair up!" Professor Stanton announced. "We're going to start sparring today. Remember, safety first! This is not a free pass to beat the crap out of each other. If I see any head shots, I'll throw you out of my class for the semester. Got it?"

"Want to spar, Helena?" Dawn asked, extending a hand for a quick shake before we started.

"Always," I smirked, shaking her hand firmly. We both ignited our hands and squared off, the air around us crackling with heat and anticipation.

"Let's do this!" Dawn taunted playfully, sending a stream of fire towards me.

"Bring it on!" I retorted, deflecting her attack with a flick of my wrist. My flames met hers head-on, creating a vibrant clash of red and orange before dissipating harmlessly into the air.

"Nice one, Helena!" Dawn smirked as a deluge of flames erupted from both of her hands toward me. "But I'm not through with you yet!"

"Ha! I'm not either!" I jumped out of the way before launching a powerful barrage of fireballs at Dawn.

She dodged and weaved, avoiding the majority of them but taking a glancing blow to the shoulder.

"Damn!" she exclaimed, rubbing the singed spot gingerly. "You've gotten faster!"

"I have. Do you think you can keep up?"

"Challenge accepted!" Dawn grinned, launching her own counterattack.

As our sparring match continued, I noticed the subtle improvements in my control and finesse. My movements were more fluid, my aim more precise. With each passing day, I felt the bond between myself and these crazy powers within me grow stronger.

"Excellent work today, everyone," Professor Stanton declared as the session came to an end. "Keep practicing and remember—control is key."

As I wiped the sweat from my forehead and the other students began to leave, the professor approached me.

"Helena, great job out there," he said. "Didn't I tell you that you're a natural?"

"You did." I chuckled.

"Don't let this go to your head but, some of the techniques you're able to execute usually take months—sometimes even an entire year—for first-year students to learn."

"Wow, I had no idea. I would've never made it this far without your help."

"After discussing your progress with another professor, she mentioned that she also has a student who is excelling at a faster pace compared to the rest of the class. She suggested that you and her student do additional training together to keep yourselves challenged."

"That sounds great!" I said, swelling with excitement and pride at the opportunity. "I've already been putting in extra training, so it'll be nice to work with someone instead of doing it on my own."

"Excellent. I'll let Professor Skogen know and we'll coordinate." Professor Stanton smiled warmly. "Keep pushing yourself, Helena. You're well on your way to being one of the top-ranked students here if you keep it up!"

"Thank you, Professor," I replied, feeling a deep sense of gratitude. "I'll do my best."

"I know you will."

Apparently, word quickly spread about my rapid progress in training and the strength of my powers compared to my peers. Later that day, Iris and I strolled through the corridors of the academy when a voice hollered, "Drake!"

I shifted my gaze towards the sound, certain that I recognized the voice, and spotted Jimmy with a wide grin on his face as he and Dawn made his way to us.

Curious, I raised an eyebrow at him. "Who's Drake?"

"You are silly," Dawn chimed in.

"Now that you mention it," I said thoughtfully, "I've been hearing people say 'Drake' all day. I just assumed they were talking to some guy named 'Drake'."

Jimmy and Dawn laughed.

"But why am I 'Drake'?" I asked, still confused.

"It's a compliment!" Iris explained. "It means *The Dragon*!"

"Because you're a badass fire-breathing dragon!" Dawn threw a dramatic fist in the air.

"I'm not sure I like it," I admitted with a slight frown. "I'm a monster?"

"No!" Iris assured. "It's a sign of respect!"

"Really?" I smiled, now feeling both flattered and amused by the nickname. "I guess that's kind of cool."

"Kind of cool?" Jimmy laughed. "It's awesome!"

"You should be proud, Helena!" Dawn said.

It was weird. My goal had always been to fly under the radar at school because my big mouth often got me into trouble. I'd never been popular before, let alone popular in the way where, suddenly, people would whisper *nice things* about me when I walked by. It was kind of overwhelming.

A couple of days later, I headed to the gym to meet with Professor Stanton. He was going to introduce me to Professor Skogen and her student so we could start training together.

"There's my prodigy!" Professor Stanton called out when I entered, then chuckled. "I heard they're calling you 'Drake' now."

"Yeah . . ." I shook my head. "It's embarrassing."

"It should be an honor!" He beamed. "You ready to get started?"

"Yes, please!"

"As I mentioned before, Professor Skogen and I both believe that it would be beneficial for you to train with her student. So, we thought the best way to test your compatibility would be through a friendly duel."

"A duel?" I asked, imagining two men swinging swords at each other in medieval times. "Like, you want me to fight?"

"No, it's just like sparring in class . . . but more formal," he corrected me with amusement. "We'll have a few more rules."

I nodded. I'd sparred several times in class, so I ought to be fine.

Professor Stanton grinned widely at me. "Great! Let's do this!"

He led me across the gym to the opposite of where we usually trained.

A very tall woman—like eight feet tall—stood waiting for us and . . . him. The gorgeous Ice Enchanted who always glared at me. Fannar.

*I'm sparring **him**?!*

I was brought alongside Professor Stanton, and he smiled and bowed lightly to the woman.

"Professor Skogen," he said politely, "how are you today?"

She smiled back at him—she had tusks.

"Good," she said, her voice a throaty growl, like Mongolian throat-singing was her regular speaking voice. "Is she ready?"

"I believe so."

"Good," Professor Skogen said. "It has been a while since Fannar has had a true challenge." Her gaze swept over me as if sizing me up. "A Fire Enchanted should be exactly what he needs."

"Great!" Professor Stanton replied cheerfully, then nudged me, "Come on, Helena! Let's get ready!"

He led me over to the other side of the mat. "Now," he said firmly, "above the belt only, and no head shots on a first spar."

"So . . . wait, what am I actually doing?" I asked.

"Simply put, you're both going to stand on this large mat and fling your powers at each other," he explained. "Just aim for his torso and not his head or below the belt. You remember the fireballs we were working on?"

"Yeah . . ." I murmured, unsurely. "But what if I hurt him?"

"It'll be fine. Fannar is strong enough to handle it. He'll be alright, and he won't be trying to hurt you either."

"Okay, but shouldn't we wear safety gear or something?"

"No, it restricts your movement too much. Plus, we have healers if anything happens." Professor Stanton patted me on the back. "This isn't a win/lose match, and you're not looking to *win*. Just trying to work out a bit. Don't be nervous. It's going to be fine. I think you're going to enjoy it. Go get 'em!"

Finally, I walked onto the mat, and Fannar faced me about twenty feet away. He had that same look in his eyes as the first day I met him—that cold, disdainful glare.

But at least it wasn't the look he'd given me the first time I used my powers in public—that icy, burning hatred. If he had been looking at me like that, then I would be fairly sure he was trying to kill me.

That was when the professor blew the whistle to start the match.

Fannar's eyes darkened to a sapphire blue and gleamed. He swung his arm toward me and pointed icicles emerged from the floor. In a second, white shards rocketed toward my face. I screamed. Darted to one side. A veritable iceberg rose into the air next to my head, then crashed down onto the mat, shattering into a million pieces.

"Damn it!" I yelped.

"Language!" Professor Skogen scolded me, but then looked at Fannar and nodded.

Fannar didn't say a word, but after looking at his mentor, he swept his arms wide. A huge wave of snow rose and then formed into little snowballs. Then, the snowballs shot toward me at the speed of a bullet.

One hit me in the thigh. Hard. The sting shuddered down my leg, and it went completely numb.

"Shit!" I howled.

"Language!" Professor Skogen snapped again from the sides.

Quick footsteps crashed toward me. I screamed and tried to limp away, but I wasn't faster than Fannar could sprint.

Clubs of ice were clenched in his fists, and as he came close, he swung. The white bludgeon rocketed toward my face. I shrieked and ducked.

Then, Fannar hissed something. "Come on! Do something!"

"Wha-what?" I gasped.

"Don't just stand there! Use your powers! Do something!" he snapped. "If someone attacks you, they won't be this easy on you."

He spoke quietly, and over his shoulder, I saw Professor Skogen scowl. He noticed her and then stepped back from me, swinging his second ice club.

My powers boiled in my panic. My hand snapped up to my face.

The ice hit my palm but hissed and melted as soon as it contacted my skin.

Fannar stepped back, but there was something in his eyes. A change. Maybe even the ghost of a smile flickered across his handsome face.

Then he stepped into a wide stance, rooted his feet into the mat, and pressed his hands together. As I watched him get into such an aggressive stance, my powers boiled in my belly in response. Then, Fannar thrust his hands forward, and a jet of ice soared through the air.

I channeled my powers through my arms and thrust my own hands forward. An explosion of fire burst out, roaring to defend me.

The fire and ice clashed with a vicious hiss. The two of them wrestled with each other but didn't get anywhere. Occasionally, the ice wheezed, and the jet of fire pushed more toward Fannar. But then he'd narrow his eyes, and the fire would give a gasp as the beam of ice pushed through toward me.

The encroaching ice was starting to drain me. I couldn't keep this up!

I looked around. There was space on either side of me, and I was sure I could get away, but only if I could keep the ice at bay.

Alright . . . here we go!

I pushed out one more powerful blast of fire—pushing away some of the ice—and then threw myself to the left, out of the way. I'd thrown myself so hard that I landed flat on my belly, winding myself. The ice beam *cracked* into the wall behind me.

I scrambled to get my knees under me and then forced myself to stand. I gasped to cram as much air into my body as I could before I passed out. My ribs ached. My heart hammered. Sweat drenched my forehead.

But then I saw Fannar. He was sweating and panting as well, hands on his knees. The duel paused for a long second as both of us gasped for a moment. We locked eyes, and I saw just a touch of playfulness in his expression.

"Ready to yield?" he called to me, somewhat breathlessly.

"Oh, please!" I snapped back, "You'd love that, wouldn't you?"

The mentors chuckled.

Fannar recovered first. He swung his hands forward, and a sheet of ice spread over the mat. Then he began skating on the ice, approaching me faster than he ever could do while he was running.

But I was ready this time. I held my hands out, a ball of fire forming in my palms. It shot out at my command, right toward Fannar. He skated away to the side, the fireball missing him by inches. He then straightened and skated right at me.

I formed a second shot and fired it at him. He was heading straight toward me, gliding effortlessly over the ice. He skidded and threw himself to one side as a fireball soared past him. I started running, eyes fixed on him as he summoned a glittering icicle in his palm. I forced another fireball into my palm as I ran around. I kept my eye on him, and I sprinted, aiming with my next fireball to—

My feet hit a patch of slippery ice and slid out from under me. I was suddenly airborne. Weightless.

I yelped. Hit the floor. Tumbled. A sting rang through my shoulder and head. I kept flailing. I tried to stand as I rolled and—

CRACK.

I heard it before I felt it. A breathtaking shudder of pain from my ankle. I finally stopped tumbling, but I wasn't getting up again. I screamed, my hands moving to my foot. It was facing an odd angle, and my ankle was quickly swelling. I cried out helplessly in pain, my eyes stinging as tears ran down my face.

Hands were suddenly on me. A voice spoke to me, but my pulse was hammering in my ears, and I couldn't hear them properly. My vision was wavering.

Something freezing pressed my ankle, numbing a little of the agony.

I looked up to see what it was—it was Fannar. His hands gently rested on my ankle, with his beautiful face crumpled in worry.

He's . . . worried? About me?

The pain kept ricocheting through my leg in unbelievable agony.

I had to distract myself. I studied his face since he was the only thing I could see at that moment.

Like ice itself, his face was both completely white and sharp. A sharp nose, a defined jawline, and those glacial blue eyes were the only color on him. His hair was only slightly whiter than the rest of his face. It was hard to tell if you weren't looking closely.

But he was just as beautiful no matter how close or far I was. Just . . . ethereally beautiful. Like a spirit. Or even an angel.

Especially when he had that look on his face, that gentle concern, his eyebrows knitting together and his face softening.

After a moment, Fannar seemed to realize I was staring at him and turned those soft blue eyes to me. "Does it hurt?" he murmured.

Suddenly, I was breathless. I didn't know whether it was because of the pain or . . .

"Not as much . . . anymore," I whispered. "Thanks."

He didn't exactly smile at me, but his face was still soft.

"No problem," he answered.

The other mentors came over.

"Damn!" Professor Stanton said. "That was quite a fall! Are you okay, Helena?"

"She's not," Fannar replied before I could. "Her ankle's broken."

"Fannar," Professor Skogen said as she inspected my ankle, "take her to the Healing Center and don't leave her until she is in the nurse's care."

"Yes, Professor Skogen."

Before I could say a word, I was taken up into Fannar's arms and pressed against his near-burningly cold body. I wrapped one of my arms around his neck for extra support, though his athletically defined biceps around me felt strong and comforting with each step he took. The places where his skin touched mine sent shivers through me, but it only made me want to lean in closer to him. I tried to ignore how fast he was making my heart beat as he carried me through the gym, all eyes on us.

CHAPTER FIVE

As Fannar carried me through the gym, students turned to stare at us. Those in the middle of duels stopped and pointed at us. Murmurs rose from all around. Even the mentors looked at us from the corner of their eyes and raised their eyebrows.

I knew that both Fannar and I had drawn attention to ourselves—with him being the top student and me rising in the ranks so quickly—but I hadn't thought the sight of us together was going to raise such a ruckus.

But, apparently, the sight of Fannar carrying me in his arms was the most exciting thing they had ever seen. Students whispered as we passed by. I got the sense that even the mentors were going to have a little chat about this later.

Being pressed against Fannar's chest, I grumbled, "I'm sorry. This is so embarrassing . . ."

Fannar's polar eyes darted down to me and back up. The frostiness was back.

"It is fine," he said under his breath, his voice monotone.

He got to the gym door and shoved it open with his shoulder. We burst out into the corridor in front of more faces than I could count.

So many wide eyes and whispers as we passed them. Fannar gave an annoyed sound at the back of his throat at all the attention, but when I looked at his face, there was no emotion in his expression at all. I could tell he was upset since I was pressed against him, but he was expertly hiding it from everyone else.

When we got to the Healing Center, Fannar leaned into the doors again, easing them open. The Healing Center looked less like a medical clinic and more like someone had set up a dozen beds inside of a historic castle. The dark gray walls were made of rough stone, and huge arched windows let in natural light.

A nurse in a long dress approached us. She looked like a typical nurse, but her arms were the spiked limbs of a praying mantis.

"Well, don't you have a lovely bride?" the nurse teased. Fannar bristled a bit, but I was just happy that her demeanor didn't match her scary arms. "What happened?"

I opened my mouth to respond, but Fannar was faster. "I think her ankle is broken," he replied.

"Name?"

"Helena," he said.

She scribbled on a clipboard. "You're going to wait for a bit. The healer is dealing with a concussed student right now."

She looked up at Fannar. "Can you stay with her until the healer can see her?"

He nodded.

"Great, please follow me." As she led us away, her scuttling insect legs peaked out from under her dress.

She directed us into a little private side room and gestured to the bed. Fannar walked inside and placed me down carefully. He started by placing my back down first, then gently lowered my legs until they rested on the bed. He was so cautious, but the moment my broken ankle landed, I gave a light cry.

"Oh, gods! I'm so sorry!" Fannar said.

Again, the icy facade dropped a little, his eyes shining with concern. It was like he was a different person when he looked at me like that.

"It's okay. It is just . . . delicate."

The mantis nurse gave me a sympathetic look, and Fannar sat in the chair next to the bed.

"That's a nasty break you got there. I'll bring the healer as soon as he's done with the other kid."

She then turned and left.

I looked back to Fannar. His cold mask had come back, and he didn't have any expression on his face.

I gestured to my ankle. "So, does this happen a lot to people who duel you?"

Fannar's eyes flickered up at me. "No," he answered. "Most people are more careful about not slipping on ice when they are fighting an Ice Enchanted."

"Funny."

I tried to come up with something witty to say, but nothing came. Awkward silence reigned for a bit.

"So . . . what year are you?" I asked, the silence driving me crazy.

Again, it took Fannar a long time to answer, like he was debating with himself whether he should answer me.

"I'm a second year."

"Cool. How do you like it so far?"

Fannar shrugged, looking away from me.

There was another long silence. I hated silence and had a nasty habit of trying to fill it with small talk.

"What are you going to do after the academy?" I asked. "Like, once you've graduated?"

Fannar just gave a small bitter laugh. He didn't answer otherwise. He barely met my eye, like he was looking everywhere *but* at me. When he accidentally met my gaze, he soon broke it, looking somewhere else.

I watched him look around for a long, silent moment. The iciness from him saturated the air and chilled me to the bone.

"Why don't you like me?" I asked him, breaking the silence. "What did I do to make you hate me?"

Fannar looked at me fully for the first time in a solid minute, frowning hard.

"I didn't say I hated you," he replied.

"You don't need to say it," I retorted. "You've made it pretty damn clear." It had sounded a lot stronger and more accusatory in my head, but the pain from my ankle made it come out whinier than I had intended. However, it seemed to spark something in him. His eyes softened a little.

"Sorry, but it's nothing personal," he said. "It's just nature."

"What do you mean 'nature'?" I asked, slightly insulted. "Because I was born in the Unenchanted Realm?"

"No." He shook his head. "You're Fire and I'm Ice. We're natural enemies. I'm not even supposed to be talking to you."

I could only blink for a moment at the absurdity of someone telling a grown adult that they can't speak to another grown adult. "Who said you're not supposed to?"

Now, he was frowning again. "Everyone. It's just the way things are here."

"Well, I haven't been at this academy for as long as you, but we're probably the two highest-ranking students, so we're probably going to be paired together in duels a lot."

"So?"

"If we're going to be dueling a lot, shouldn't we talk like civilized people outside of duels?"

He shrugged. "Fire and Ice don't mix."

"What if I'm not just Fire, though?" I asked. "What if I'm Fire *and* Ice? What then?"

Fannar stiffened as if I'd just uttered a secret or said something that could have me arrested. He seemed to freeze over for a long moment before regaining his composure. "That's not possible," he retorted with annoyance.

"Oh, really?" I knew I had to show him, or he wouldn't believe me. I pulled the collar of my gym shirt down to show the area under my collarbone. Fannar looked alarmed.

"What are you doing?" His eyes darted around to see if anyone was watching.

I held my hand over my collarbone and revealed my Enchanted mark of the volcano with a snowflake inside of it.

He stood up from the chair, and a hundred expressions crossed his face in a second—awe, fear, anger, confusion, wonder—before he finally settled on suspicion. "That's not real!"

"It is!" I promised. "Look!" I put two fingers over it and rubbed it hard, dragging my skin back and forth to show it wasn't simply drawn on there.

I jumped suddenly as an icy hand pressed against my clavicle, spreading a chill to my bones. His pale fingers were gentle but firm, tracing the lines of the mark with a curious and inquisitive touch. My whole body tensed from the delectable cold as he brushed my skin.

When I looked down, Fannar's face was *so* close to mine as he examined my mark.

"That's impossible . . ." he murmured.

I couldn't help but run my eyes over his beautiful face, but then I noticed his other hand was clutching his own collarbone over his shirt, where his mark would be.

"Fannar," I said quietly, immediately suspicious, "let me see your mark."

He stood up straight and looked at me, his eyes worried, but he slowly pulled down his shirt collar.

Instinctively, I reached out and pressed my hand to his collarbone. The coolness of his skin sent a chilly ripple through my body. When I raised my hand, there was a snowflake with a volcano inside of it.

"My parents told me it shouldn't look like that, that I should never let anyone see it," he explained, letting go of his collar to cover the mark with his shirt again.

"But you don't have fire powers?" I asked.

"No," he breathed. "Do you have any ice?"

"Not that I know of."

He bent down to look at my mark again as it faded away, and then glanced at me, those frigid eyes drilling deeply into me.

"What does this mean?" he murmured, his lips just an inch from mine.

"I—"

The door behind Fannar opened, and he snapped straight up, away from me. The mantis nurse came back in.

"The healer is ready for her now."

Fannar nodded and walked out of the door before I could say a word.

CHAPTER SIX

As badly fractured as my ankle was, it only took about an hour for me to be healed. But an hour was enough time for Fannar to disappear on me.

For the next two weeks, we went back to our old patterns—me with Iris and Fannar with his other friends, only being face-to-face when we trained—except even frosty Fannar couldn't hide the change in his eyes. Before, he used to glare at me with a narrowed gaze, eyes burning with disdain. But after my injury, his gaze had softened. A lot. He looked like he wanted to talk to me, but he didn't have the nerve.

Based on what he'd said before, I assumed he didn't want people talking about us because of that silly Fire and Ice business, but, if he was worried about other people's opinions, he didn't show it. I couldn't be the only one who noticed him staring at me every second he got the chance.

Iris and I walked through the main hallway on our way to our next class, history of the Enchanted Realm, when I felt the familiar burning of Fannar's gaze. As always, those icy eyes caught me and held me from across the room. They were boundless, like they could hold me forever if something never broke his gaze. It reminded me of a completely clear and endless lake, shining crystalline blue.

He looked away when one of his friends gestured to him. Fannar shared one more lingering glance with me before leaving.

Iris nudged me with her elbow and said, "We need to go or we're going to be late." She gave me a cheeky grin as she led me further down the hall.

"What?" I asked.

"What's going on between you and Fannar? Everyone's talking about it."

"Yeah, I bet they are," I grumbled.

"You guys had that duel a while ago, and then he's suddenly carrying you in his arms like newlyweds—"

"My ankle was broken!" I protested.

Iris's cheeky grin grew wider. "*Sure*," she teased. "But that doesn't explain why you guys are always staring at each other like you're both hypnotized. Are you two together?"

For a second, I was back in the Healing Center again, remembering how close Fannar's face was to mine as he inspected my Enchanted mark. Then, I shuddered and came back to reality.

"No!" I exclaimed. "We're not even *friends*."

Iris laughed softly.

"Come on! The Ice Prince doesn't melt for just anybody!"

I rolled my eyes. "Ha! If he's a prince, he's definitely not charming!"

Iris paused, and her lips thinned to a thoughtful line.

"What?" I asked.

"Uh," she began, "you know he's an actual prince, right? As in, heir to the Ice Kingdom?"

"Wait, what?!"

She laughed. "You seriously didn't know? You picked a prince!"

Is that why he scoffed when I asked him what he was doing after graduating?

"No." I shook my head. "I'm from the Unenchanted Realm, remember?" I wondered if Fannar being the prince of the Ice Kingdom had something to do with him not being allowed to talk to me. "So," I said after a second, "do the kingdoms get along?"

Iris gave a nervous laugh. "Oh, gods, no. To be honest, they've been on the brink of war since . . . well, since before

I was born. Before my mom was born, I think. Maybe longer."

"All of them at the brink of war with each other? Seriously?"

Iris shrugged, wincing a little. "Uh . . . it's kind of complicated. Politically, I mean. The Storm and Earth Kingdoms have been at odds over their boundaries. At least, that's what I think they're fighting about."

"And let me guess, Fire and Ice aren't so chummy either."

Iris gave another anxious laugh. "Definitely not! They're even *worse!*"

"It's not just a 'you're Fire, I'm Ice' thing, is it?"

"No, that kind of came after the Fire Princess was killed."

"Oh, right. That'd probably do it, wouldn't it?"

"Yeah," Iris replied, "I don't know the details, but the Fire Princess was killed, and the Fire Kingdom blamed the Ice Enchanted. Of course, the Ice Kingdom denied it, and no one was ever brought to justice, so things haven't been great since. I mean, Storm and Earth were at a stalemate while they argued territories, but Fire and Ice had been taking shots at each other for a while—an assassination here, a blown-up building there. It's not great."

"Yeah . . ." I murmured. "I can imagine."

When Fannar said that *everyone* knew that Fire and Ice don't mix, could it be that it wasn't the students he was referring to but his own kingdom? If he was seen with a Fire Enchanted, it might make things politically complicated. It didn't make it any less wrong, but I suddenly felt like I was getting some insight into where he was coming from.

"So why are all of you here from different kingdoms if you're basically at war with each other?" I asked.

"It's been a tradition for hundreds of years. The academies are neutral territory, so they are the one place where all Enchanted coexist. Headmaster Moira says that the academies are the greatest chance for peace between the kingdoms. Spending time with people who are different from us builds understanding. Eventually, she hopes we'll become leaders of our kingdoms and turn that understanding into peace. It's an inspiring mission."

"Yeah, that is pretty cool." I nodded.

If the goal of the academy was to help the kingdoms reconcile through their children, it seemed like the perfect place for Fannar and me to become friends. After all, Iris and I were friends, despite being in different guilds and whatever differences our kingdoms might have with each other.

That was it. It was now my personal mission to become friends with Fannar. Not just because I wanted to, and because *he* clearly wanted to, but because it could be a great example to the Enchanted Realm that someone started building that bridge between kingdoms. It was worth a try, right?

"Helena, we need to hurry! We're almost late to class!" Iris pulled at my arm, breaking me from my revolutionary thoughts.

After history, Iris and I walked to our next class together. She looked pale and bug-eyed. "I can't believe exams are coming up *so* fast!"

"You'll be fine," I comforted. "You've worked really hard."

"I never feel like it's enough," she whined.

I tried to give her a comforting pat on the back, but then I felt it again, that same arctic gaze on me.

When I looked up, of course, it was Fannar, leaning against the wall, surrounded by friends. While his friends were talking to each other, Fannar was looking at me.

Well, now's as good a time as any.

"Iris," I said, "I need to talk to Fannar for a sec."

Her worries about the upcoming exams disappeared instantly. Her head did a neck-snapping jolt, and she stared up at me, eyes bugging even more. "What?! But I thought you two weren't friends!"

*Not friends, **yet**.*

"We're not, but I have to ask him something."

"Well," Iris said, "I'll wait here, then."

I nodded and turned away, her gaze burning into the back of my head as I did.

She was not the only one staring. As I walked toward Fannar and his friends, his eyes widened as I boldly strode up to him. One of his friends elbowed Fannar in the ribs and smirked as I approached, whispering "Drake" under his breath. The softness in Fannar's eyes froze over defensively.

"Hey," I greeted him as confidently as I could pretend.

Fannar's eyes narrowed a little. "What do *you* want?" That chilly tone was back, which I expected, given we were surrounded by his ice gang.

"Professor Stanton said I need more practice before my mid-term exam, and I *really* don't want to fail my first semester. You're the only one worth sparring around here, so . . . do you have time to spar with me?"

Okay, so maybe Stanton didn't say I needed more practice, nor was I anywhere close to failing, but you can never practice too much, right?

Fannar's eyebrows rose as he thought about it. His friends, however, looked a bit offended.

I stared back at them, fully facing them, my hand sliding to my hip as I stared down the guy standing closest to Fannar. "What? You want to spar with me instead, snow boy?"

"You don't, Aspen," Fannar said quickly, his eyes sparkling with a small laugh. "You really don't. Fine. I have a meeting tonight, but I can do it tomorrow. I'll meet you at five o'clock in the gym after my session with Professor Skogen and kick your ass."

I gave him a playful smile as I turned away.

"Don't break anything this time," he scoffed.

"The only thing I'll be breaking is you!" I sneered back.

He gave a single low chuckle as I walked away.

CHAPTER SEVEN

The next day passed with little fanfare—I got up, worked on my powers a bit more with Professor Stanton, then got some extra reading done in the library before I had to meet with Fannar in the gym at five o'clock.

When I got to the gym, a few students were still staying late to train, but it was nowhere near the number of people it had during the day. I found a mat in the corner far away from anyone else and waited. After a while, Fannar still hadn't shown. I walked in circles. I wrung my hands. My heart raced in my chest.

Just as I started to lose hope, though, a ghost-white figure walked in, a gym bag slung over his broad shoulders.

I lifted my arms over my head and waved. "Hey! Fannar!"

He looked up at me and lifted a hand in greeting. He did, in fact, smile. Just a little. But . . . it was a sad smile. A resigned smile. Tired. Exhausted.

Something's bothering him.

As he walked up to me, even his usual gliding movement was hampered by exhaustion. He almost looked unwell.

Fannar stopped and gave another tight smile.

"Right," he grunted lightly. "You wanted to spar?"

"Yeah," I murmured, "but . . . are you okay? You look . . ."

I shrugged. Fannar nodded with that same tight smile.

"I'm tired," he said curtly. "You want to practice or not?"

"Yeah," I replied. "If you're up for it."

He nodded, then placed his bag down on the floor.

"What are the rules?" he sighed.

"Um, same as the exam will be, right? Powers and hand to hand. Headshots allowed, no below the belt."

Fannar nodded. "Right."

He took his shoes off and then walked and stood at the opposite end of the mat from me. He bounced on his toes a few times and nodded.

I nodded back, and a ball of flame appeared in my hands.

Fannar swept an arm upward, and a sheet of ice appeared below my feet. It swirled beneath my feet, but I was prepared.

I channeled my powers into the soles of my feet, and the ice dispersed from under me—just in time for large spikes to sprout around me.

I flung a fireball through the spikes, and Fannar leaped out of the way. A ramp of snow formed over my head. The spikes had trapped me. I summoned fire into my palms and pressed them against one of the spikes. The icicle hissed and melted in my hands, then I leaned back and kicked it. Half of the ice spike shattered and fell apart.

I sprinted away—just in time to hear a *crack* behind me.

Too slow! I cheered in my head.

I spun around and saw Fannar with his fist stuck in the ice. He pulled his hand out with another large *crack* and stood before me.

I needed to strike first.

Sprinting forward on the ice, I launched a roundhouse kick at his head. Fannar threw an arm up and blocked my kick. He stepped back, and as my leg hit the floor, I was up in his face. I threw a left hook, and he caught it. I threw a jab right at his nose.

It landed. His head rocked back, and he stumbled.

I landed one!

Fannar waved an arm and spread more ice across the floor. He skated away, putting more distance between us.

My powers surged in my stomach as I thrust both my palms forward.

Two large streams of flame erupted from my hands, and Fannar paused. I didn't know why he paused, but he looked like a deer in headlights.

Then the jets of flame hit him—right in the chest.

He shouted in pain, falling backward and sliding a few feet on his side.

To my horror, a streak of blood coated the ice. I gasped and ran to him. He was usually quick to get back on his feet, so my worry grew at how slowly he was getting up.

"Are you okay?" I asked.

"Ugh!" he gave a frustrated grunt as he sat up. Blood dripped down his bicep.

"You're bleeding!"

"It's just a scratch," he said, examining his wound. "It'll stop in a second."

He was right. The blood crystallized into frozen droplets as it contacted his icy skin.

"Are you okay?" I repeated. "I've never been able to hit you like that before."

Fannar looked at the ground.

I sat down next to him on the cold mat. "What's wrong with you?" I pressed again. "I can tell there's something wrong."

When I said that, Fannar's face softened more than I'd ever seen. It was like he'd never heard those words before, somehow. He sighed a little, then looked around. When I followed his gaze, he was looking at the others in the gym. They hadn't noticed us, but he watched them worriedly.

"Hey," I said softly, "I think we're both ready for the physical exam, but I could use some help on Enchanted Realm history."

Fannar considered for a moment, then offered, "I actually have some notes from last year that might help. We can go get them from the library."

"Sounds good. I think I've done enough sparring today."

He stood up and looked at the scrape on his arm again.

"Is it still bleeding?" I asked.

"No. It's fine," he answered.

"Okay," I replied, "just as long as you're okay."

We hadn't been in the gym together for very long, but something about Fannar's expression already seemed a bit warmer.

"Thanks," he muttered.

The library was much more crowded than the gym was. It was filled wall to wall with students, all with their noses in books, yet with very little chatter.

"This way." Fannar gave me a little nudge. "I have a study room."

Before I could say anything, he quickly led me through the library—striding through with a powerful walk. Again, he seemed to keep an eye on everyone else, very aware of where they were looking. Luckily, no one seemed to care. We were just another pair of footsteps interrupting their study.

A series of small study rooms lined one side of the library. The one at the end was completely dark and empty, and Fannar took out a set of keys from his pocket to unlock the door.

"You . . . have your own key to a study room in the library?" I asked.

"My parents paid for extra privacy," Fannar replied quietly.

He opened the door and walked in. When I followed him and closed the door, the lock clicked into place behind us.

It was a cozy and intimate space, the perfect environment for one to three students to study in peace or hold conversations, all without disturbing other students.

The room was rectangular, with one large window that overlooked the library's manicured exterior grounds. The beige plastic blinds were noticeably drawn for extra privacy. Aside from a large blank whiteboard and an array of colorful markers, the walls were bare.

The overhead fluorescent light was switched off, casting the long wooden table and three black office-style chairs into darkness. It was perfect for long hours of studying. The table was covered with stacks of books and notebooks, a couple of pens, and a single desk lamp, which seemed to be Fannar's preferred method of lighting. A tiny fridge hummed in one corner, so he didn't even need to leave the room to get a cold drink.

"Must be nice to be a rich royal, huh?" I remarked.

Fannar rolled his eyes and didn't respond. He began shuffling through some notebooks on the table, looking for the notes he had promised me.

"So, what's bothering you?" I asked him. "It's obvious that something's wrong."

Fannar continued to rifle through his notebooks as he spoke. "Why do you care?"

It was an honest question, the first I'd heard from him that completely lacked defensiveness.

I thought about it for a second.

"I know you have this too-cool-for-you attitude going on, but you were nice to me when I broke my ankle, so I think you're actually a decent person. And I still think we can be friends, by the way."

"Hm," Fannar mumbled, stopping his search.

I tapped my foot. "I'm not leaving until you tell me."

Fannar sighed and sat in a chair. He looked off at a random spot on the wall as if debating whether to speak. I sat across from him and waited. Finally, he looked at me, and there was an intensity in his eyes that I couldn't quite decipher.

"Helena, in the Unenchanted Realm, do they marry women off to men they don't want to marry?"

"What?" I asked.

He just stared at me, waiting for me to answer.

"Uh, not where I'm from, no. People don't think that's okay anymore. Why?"

He finally spoke—and this time, it was like a dam had burst. He spoke not like he wanted to, but like he had to. "*Exactly!* It was so wrong! *So* wrong, and somehow *no one sees it!* How does no one see how wrong it is around here?!"

He was on the verge of screaming. I got up from the opposite side of the table and sat next to him, though it did little to quiet him down. He kept going. "How can they give Gwyneira over to someone like she's some cow at the market and *no one cares?!*"

Fannar ran out of steam and hung his head in his hands.

"Who's Gwyneira?"

He lifted his head from his hands to look at me sadly.

"My little sister. I got a letter this morning saying that my parents finally agreed to an arranged marriage. They shipped my sister off to the Storm Kingdom to be married, and I wasn't there"—he ground his teeth for a moment before continuing—"I wasn't there to stop it. No one seems to get it. All of my friends just say that she's a princess, and that's what happens, but Brontes is a monster. After I told my parents how horrible he is, I thought they weren't going to go through with it." He sighed. "They just gave her away to the worst person I've ever met."

"Why was she betrothed to him?" I asked.

Fannar scoffed. "He's the Storm Prince. We need the Storm Kingdom as allies." He shook his head. "I'm such an idiot . . . I shouldn't have come back this semester and left her alone. This was all my fault!"

"Don't say that," I protested. "It's not your fault."

Fannar looked at me.

"You can't blame yourself for what your parents did," I added.

He was still silent for a moment. "I know . . ." He said it like a confession, looking away as if he didn't want me to see his emotions. "But I'm scared for her, Helena. He's a monster to complete strangers. How is he going to treat someone whom he thinks of as his property? But no one cares. No one *understands!*"

"Hey," I said quietly, resting my hand on his shoulder long enough to make him look at me. "I'm not going to pretend I understand all the politics or whatever between kingdoms, but it's okay to be scared for your sister. That's what a good brother does, isn't it?"

Fannar gave me a look that made me shiver—his eyes so very intense, like they were piercing straight into my soul. "Thanks, Helena," he said. "You're the only one who gets it."

I shrugged, half-smiling at him.

"What about your parents?" he asked. "Are they as heartless as mine?"

I paused, considering how much I should reveal. Often when people discovered that I was an orphan, they often became overly sympathetic and treated me differently, as if something was wrong with me. But then I remembered how much he had opened up to me and felt like I owed him the same honesty.

"No, my parents were wonderful," I began. "But they died when I was twelve . . . in a car accident."

Fannar's expression softened. "I'm sorry, Helena. I had no idea."

"It's okay," I said, forcing a smile. "I went into the foster system after that. They never even told me about my powers. All I have left of them is a wooden music box that I've had since I could remember."

"I'm so sorry." He reached out and put his hand over mine. A chill crawled through my body as his icy skin met mine. My chest clenched. My breath shuddered a little. His fingers slowly wrapped around my hand, giving it a little squeeze. My skin tingled from the delicate, feather-soft touch.

He gazed into my eyes and leaned closer to me. I held my breath.

At that moment, there was a loud *thud* from outside, like books being dropped on the floor. Fannar's head snapped toward the door, and he wrenched his hand from mine. He was no longer touching me, but I was still under a wintry spell.

He went back to shuffling through his notes as if nothing had happened. "Here it is." He handed me a notebook, which was opened up to a page scrawled with handwriting.

I took the notebook from him and turned to leave in a daze.

"More training tomorrow night?" he asked before I could open the door. "It'll have to be a bit later, though. How about nine o'clock?"

"Sure," I muttered breathlessly and floated out of the door.

CHAPTER EIGHT

I couldn't believe how little Fannar had to touch me to leave my head spinning. I couldn't sleep the previous night because all I could think of was his soft, icy fingers brushing over mine and his wonderful frosty-blue eyes penetrating my soul.

"Helena!" Iris jabbed me with her elbow.

"Huh?" She startled me.

"We have to get back in fifteen minutes, and you haven't eaten anything."

"Oh . . ."

I looked down at my full plate of food, then saw Frankie the chef gremlin, his red ears jutting out over the counter as he looked at me.

I pretended not to notice and started scooping potatoes into my mouth.

"You're acting weird," Iris said. The gears in her head turned, and she gave a little smirk. "Did something happen when you went to train with Fannar last night?"

I couldn't help but smirk as well.

"Yeah . . . remember when I said we weren't even friends?"

"Yes?"

"Well . . . I *think* we're friends now . . . maybe more . . . but I'm not sure, to be honest."

"What?!" Iris squeaked loudly before lowering her voice.

"We just got chatting, and not small talk either. Big talk. And he wanted to meet again tonight," I explained.

Iris's jaw dropped. "I didn't think Ice Enchanted hung out with Fire Enchanted, let alone the *prince!*"

"I don't think he's allowed to," I whispered. "So you need to keep it on the down-low, Iris. At least for now."

Her expression furrowed a little. "Of course, I will. But if people see you, they're going to talk, just like they did when you broke your ankle."

She was right. I didn't know the details of the politics in this world, but it obviously made Fannar worry, and everyone else made such a big deal out of it, so we couldn't be careless . . . *But he still wants to meet me tonight!* I thought smugly. I grinned as I finished my lunch.

At 9:00 p.m., I waited in the gym for Fannar. This time, the gym was completely empty. All the other students probably had their heads buried in homework at this time of night, as I usually would if it weren't for Fannar.

I waited.

Did he forget about me? I wondered.

I waited.

I checked the clock. 9:15. Why did it feel like forever?

"Hey!" Fannar jogged into the gym.

My head snapped up. "You're fifteen minutes late," I said, annoyed.

"Sorry, I wanted to make sure no one saw us come in together, or they—"

"Yeah, yeah, Ice Kingdom and Fire Kingdom at war. I know, I know." I rolled my eyes.

Fannar gave a half-smile and dropped his bag.

"You ready for some training?"

As he spoke, I paused to take him in. He wore his gym uniform, the shirt's breathable material pulling tight across his broad chest, every peak and valley of him very obvious in—

I shook myself out of my thoughts. "Yeah, let's do this."

"Same rules as last time?"

"Sure."

Fannar went to the other side of the mat and readied himself. I did the same on my side.

He took a lunging step forward, stomping his foot on the ground. A shield of clear ice shot up from nowhere in front of him. He side-kicked it, shattering it into pieces, and a hundred diamond-shaped missiles of ice rocketed toward me.

Two thick ribbons of flame burst from my clenched fists, and I wielded them like whips, throwing my arms back before cracking the flames forward. The fire snapped around and shattered the volley of ice.

But I was looking at them for too long—Fannar was gone!

I looked around, only to see his foot heading for my side.

The kick slammed into my ribs and hurtled my body backward a few feet. When I landed, my side ached, but I was ready for the next strike.

As Fannar stalked toward me, I formed a finger gun with both hands, intertwining my fingers together with just the index fingers and thumbs out. Time to try out a new move I'd been thinking about. I concentrated on forcing every ounce of my strength into the very tips of my index fingers.

A thin jet of white-hot flames erupted where I aimed my "fire gun". He was forced to duck out of the way of the blast and backed away from me.

We braced ourselves again, and I struck first this time, summoning a fireball before hurling it at him. Fannar dodged the attack, but I came in close.

I hurled a punch at his face, and he slipped past it, my fist glancing off his cheek as he moved away. He grabbed my fist in one hand, using his other hand to shove my shoulder and put me off balance. As I struggled to right myself, Fannar pushed me backward until my spine hit the wall.

My back against the wall, him holding one of my arms to the side, he gripped my other arm and pinned it by my waist.

He was so close to me . . . I could feel him. He wasn't radiating body heat. Instead, it was some kind of body *cold* that seemed to strengthen when our legs touched.

"Got you," he breathed. "Good thing, too. I was starting to worry that the new kid had waltzed in and upstaged me."

My entire body was tingling with delight at how close he was to me, but my competitive streak burned just a little brighter.

I used my free leg to sweep Fannar's foot, then leaned my body weight forward to knock him over. As he fell, he held onto my arms and dragged me down with him.

He landed flat on his back, and I managed to land kneeling without landing *on* him, boxing him in.

But that left my knees on either side of his hips, him underneath me.

As I straddled him, that sweet cold radiated through me from below, and it was . . . breathtaking. I'd never felt anything like it. My heartbeat turned quicker and heavier. My breath heaved.

I could barely get any words out. "Oh, yeah? Got me, have you?"

My body shivered in such anticipation that I could barely breathe, let alone move. Fannar then flashed me the most wicked grin, and he bucked his hips underneath me.

I hit the mat with a thud as Fannar flipped me onto my back. Then, that cold that was radiating through me suddenly spread over my entire body. I opened my eyes, and Fannar's face was so close, his nose almost touching mine.

I could feel his heartbeat from where his chest rested on mine, a soft cold moving over my torso. His icy breath fanned out over my face, and it felt like walking outside on a crisp winter's day for the first time. His panting breath pressed his heaving chest into mine every time he breathed in.

"Clever," he murmured. "But I've been doing this longer than you."

I didn't say anything. I never realized how *wintery* he smelled. I'd never been able to pin down what the smell of snow was, but that was what Fannar smelled like. I could have just . . . breathed it in forever.

I shivered, trying to anticipate his next move, as he gently rested on me. He was so close. There was nowhere to look but his eyes.

"Sorry." Fannar stared back into my eyes. "Are you cold?"

I shook my head quickly, not being able to answer. A light, tingling numbness from the cold was setting in, but I loved it.

"I didn't think so," he replied, his eyes never leaving mine. "You're so *warm*."

His legs settled on either side of me, and he hovered above me, bracing himself with one arm. The fingers of his other hand traced my cheek. "Your skin is hot. I've never felt anything so warm in my life . . . I could get burned . . ."

His eyes flickered down to my lips, and his face came tantalizingly closer to mine.

I couldn't take it anymore. It was starting to be painful to wait. I leaned up and kissed him.

The chill was immediate, both from his sweet lips and his breath as he gasped. I wasn't sure if it was a good gasp or a bad one, so I pulled away to read how he was feeling. Is it possible for ice to burn? Because his eyes melted me, and my face froze inches from his.

Fannar's hand moved to the back of my head and pulled me into him. His lips pressed fiercely onto mine, and the iciness of his mouth against my lips sent fire running through my veins. I moaned as our kiss deepened. The coldness of his embrace surrounded my whole body, and a shudder ran through me as his tongue hungrily explored the inner depths of my mouth.

I sighed softly as his kisses trailed down my neck until they reached my annoying shirt. I didn't want him to stop. I wanted more of him, driven by an uncontrollable urge to surrender myself completely to him.

I placed my hands on his chest and eased him back. He did, breathing heavily, wintery blue eyes scouring over me in wonder and arousal. I reached my hands to the hem of my gym shirt and ripped it over my head, throwing it aside.

Fannar gave a throaty chuckle. "Oh, this is so wrong . . *so* wrong . . ."

I knew what he meant. When his frosty hands pressed on me, squarely on my overheated skin, some kind of secret instinct in my brain screamed at me about how unnatural it was that an Ice Enchanted had his hands on me.

It felt like danger. It felt like a taboo.

And it was invigorating.

My heart raced as Fannar's hands lingered on me, as he traced the tender skin that swelled from the top of my bra. Excitement surged through me, and I could tell he was savoring the illicit feeling between us. His hands moved delicately and purposefully, like he was relishing the *wrongness* of it all.

I slipped one of my hands under his shirt. He let out a soft moan as my skin brushed his ridged stomach. Fire coursed through my body, and I basked in the feeling of his abs under my fingers. I tried to reach higher up his chest, but his shirt stopped me.

Fannar gripped the bottom of his shirt, preparing to pull it off. I panted breathlessly and tremored in pleasure already. I just wanted it off. I wanted us bare. I wanted us *together*.

But then his head snapped around, and he looked at the door as if he'd heard something. It broke the spell. Suddenly, he looked horrified.

"Oh, gods . . . what are we doing?" he hissed, his eyes awash in fear. "Someone is going to see us! Helena, your shirt!"

He grabbed it and threw it at me. It landed on my chest. Fannar stood up and straightened out his clothes in a hurry, leaving me alone on the floor.

I felt very naked—and not in the way I wanted. But I couldn't get up, my thoughts spinning. All that came out was a single word.

"Why?" I asked.

Fannar looked away from me, his icy mask firmly in place. "We can't do this. We can't *ever* do this."

My heart sank at his words, but I was desperate to reason with him. "Look, I know you think Fire and Ice aren't supposed to be together, but that's just—"

"No," he interrupted. "It's more than that. You don't understand." He looked me dead in the eye. "If my parents find out, they *will* kill you, Helena."

My chest ached. He was completely serious. His words were like a thousand knives stabbing me. My whole world was crumbling around me, and I was powerless to stop it.

"I'm sorry," he said as he turned from me and quickly shuffled away, shutting the gym door behind him. I'd never felt so cold and alone.

CHAPTER NINE

F annar hadn't spoken to me since the night we'd almost . . .

Every time I thought about him, dreamed of his enchantingly arctic skin, or relived how my body burned for him, a searing pain ached in my chest. My longing to see him consumed me.

But then again, it was October, and mid-term exams were upon us. I had barely seen Iris in the past two weeks. We'd both been up late at night, studying at different places, rolling into bed in the early mornings, and crawling out perhaps fifteen minutes before our scheduled training time with our mentors. It was intense. I'd never been great at exams to begin with, but I'd never had tests like the ones in the academy.

On the day of the training exam, Professor Stanton invited four upperclassmen to spar with us as he observed and evaluated our skills. Anxiety and excitement coursed through my veins as I watched my classmates' duel, studying their distinct styles.

Dawn moved gracefully, her body fluid and precise as she attacked. Each calculated strike flowed into another in a well-choreographed dance with formidable accuracy. Angela's style was fast and fierce. Her long, black ponytail became a blur as she lunged and parried with lightning speed. She unleashed a barrage of powerful and intense blasts, leaving her opponent little time to recover. Meanwhile, Jimmy's approach was more reckless and wild, yet somehow effective as he managed to catch his opponent off-guard despite her advanced skill.

By the time it was my turn, I figured out that my opponent would be Tobin, a third-year student, and deduced some of his go-to moves.

When Professor Stanton blew his whistle, Tobin rushed toward me, flinging fire. As the fireballs soared toward me like asteroids crashing through space, I swatted them down.

He summoned jets of flame, and I met them with my fireballs, breaking the wave of combustion heading my way.

The rest of the match went the same. There wasn't a single fire attack he threw at me that I couldn't block or deflect. But, given he had a lot more experience than I did, none of my strikes got through to him either.

Things didn't seem much better when we moved to hand-to-hand combat. More than a few times, I was smacked in the face when I really should have blocked it. He was a lot tougher than the other students in my class I'd sparred with. I knew the exam would be more difficult than our routine training sessions.

Before I felt like I could make an impact, the whistle sounded, signaling the end of the exam, and I was hustled away without any indication of whether I'd won or lost, whether I'd impressed the judges or not, or whether I'd even passed. I just hoped that I did better than the other freshmen in the Fire Guild.

After two more written exams and turning in a paper on Wednesday, the stress was finally gone, and I had a few free days to relax. Iris also finished her exams early. The following week, I found out I had passed all my exams with flying colors.

One of the amazing things about Haven Academy was that the Storm Guild kept the weather at a perfect seventy-three degrees all year round at Headmaster Moira's request. Even though it was mid-October, we were able to spend a few lazy days in the sun outside.

"Do you have a date for the Fall Dance yet?" Iris asked me as we lounged about on the grass outside.

"The dance? I haven't even thought about it, to be honest," I answered.

Iris giggled. "You might want to start thinking about it! It's at the end of next week, and you have to buy tickets ahead of time!" She brought her knees up and embraced them. "Guiden asked me to be his date to the dance," she admitted shyly.

"What?!" I exclaimed, sitting up from where I was lounging. "Who's Guiden? Have you met a boy?"

Iris looked at me, a blush rising in her pale skin, and started giggling.

"I tell you everything!" I protested playfully. "Spill it!"

Iris giggled again. "He's a guy in the Earth Guild who's in two of my classes. We've been talking, and we both like the same authors, and—and he plays the lute, and he's just . . . he's really sweet!" Iris smiled, looking off into the middle distance. "He's such a good listener. He actually pays attention to the things I say I like and remembers! On Tuesday, he made this big gesture about asking me to the dance—my favorite flowers and chocolates with a cute little message written across them." She exhaled a little dreamy sigh. "Of course, I had to say yes!"

I chucked. "I'm happy for you, but I would have hated that!"

"Really?"

"Yeah, I'm not really a flower and chocolates kind of girl. Not into that traditional romantic stuff."

Iris smiled at me. "Should I let Fannar know?" she teased.

I frowned and looked at the ground. "Yeah, I don't think that's going to make a difference."

"What?" Iris gasped. "I thought you two hit it off. What happened?"

I shrugged. "He just . . . decided that it was too dangerous."

"Oh, no! I'm sorry, Helena," Iris said sadly. She thought for a moment and suddenly became very excited. "But you can be together at the dance!"

"What do you mean?"

"Even though most of us stick to our own guild, dances are some of the few times where we're all stuffed together in one place. So, if you two were hanging out, it wouldn't be a big deal."

"Really?" I asked, cautious about getting my hopes up. Iris nodded.

"But he hasn't asked me, so I guess it doesn't matter."

Iris smiled at me. "*You* ask him! You just said you don't like all that traditional romantic stuff, anyway!"

I gave a weak chuckle. "I did say that, didn't I?" I didn't want to admit it, but the idea of looking him in the eyes after what happened was terrifying. If he rejected me again, I wouldn't be able to bear it.

"Come on!" Iris grabbed my arm.

"Where were we going?" I asked.

"We're going to find Fannar!"

Iris dragged me around the entire academy looking for Fannar, but we couldn't find him. We checked the gym, the outside, the library, and the break areas.

"Well, I guess he's in his dorm then," Iris murmured.

"Right," I replied, except I knew there was one place he could be that she didn't know about.

"Could you ask Guiden to go look for him in the boys' dorms?"

"Oh," Iris's eyes sparkled at the idea of having a reason to talk to Guiden. "Sure, I'll go ask him."

"Sounds good. I'll keep looking around, and we'll meet up here later."

She nodded and trotted off.

I turned and started toward the library, heading straight to his private study room. As I approached it, I could see a dim light underneath the door. *He's here!*

My heart anxiously raced as I knocked. There was a soft shuffle, then the door opened.

And he was there, just as gorgeous as the first time I saw him. His hair and skin were like fresh snow on the peak of a mountain. His piercing blue eyes were endlessly deep.

For a moment, my anxiety melted as I took him in . . . until he furrowed his brow at the sight of me.

Fannar stuck his head out of the doorway to take a quick glance around and then grabbed my hand, pulling me into the room. "Hurry, come in before someone sees you!"

The door shut and locked behind us. Once we were alone in the dark together, his frosty hand still on mine, I could feel the chills passing between us. I leaned forward, just a little, and felt the line of his body rest against mine and the cold radiating from his entire body.

His breathing changed. Just a little heavier than before.

My eyes adjusted to the darkness, and I saw his eyes burning into me, moving slowly from my eyes to my lips and back. I seriously considered leaning up to kiss him, but Fannar gently let my hand go and walked away from me.

"What are you doing here, Helena?" he asked, almost annoyed. "I told you, it's dangerous."

Fannar went over to the table, which was cluttered with open books. I had interrupted his studying.

"I know . . ." I started, as my nerves rose back up. "Did you hear about the dance?"

"What about it?" he asked, a forced calm in his voice.

"Well, Iris said that everyone from different guilds will be hanging out together . . . so it won't be a big deal if people see us together?" I wasn't sure how my statement had become a question.

His eyes looked up at me, but he kept his face turned toward the book in front of him. "Are you . . . asking me to the dance?"

"Ummm, yeah. If you want to go."

Fannar paused, his expression unreadable.

"Do you want to go?" I asked him after a while.

Fannar was still quiet. Did I mention that I hated silence?

"I mean . . ." I trailed off. I was having trouble finding the words. My stomach was wobbling, my heart was hammering, and this was already not going the way I had hoped.

"I miss you," I blurted out suddenly with desperation in my voice that I didn't expect.

Fannar looked at his book and closed his eyes. Again, he said nothing for a long time.

A wave of dread passed through me, dread at what he would say next after I let myself be so vulnerable to him yet again. But it was far worse to wait in agony for his response.

"Say something, please!" I pleaded.

His eyes finally locked on mine, glowing with sadness.

"Helena, I miss you, too. But we *can't* be together. It's not that I don't *want* to. It's that we *can't*."

My heart nearly stopped beating. "But everyone at the dance will be from different guilds," I reasoned as I tried to push my emotions, and tears, down. "It won't be a big deal."

"I'm not worried about our classmates making it a big deal. I'm worried that one of them will open their big mouth and my parents find out their Ice Prince is with a Fire Enchanted."

"They wouldn't dare try something at the academy though, right?"

"My parents hate the Fire Kingdom with a passion. If they find out how I feel about you, they would risk it. They *will* try to kill you." He looked at me more sternly. "You have to stop. We can't do this, any of this."

It felt like a knife had been thrust into my heart . . . not from fear that his parents might try to kill me but the crushing pain of believing that he didn't think I was worth fighting for. Now, my eyes were stinging fully. I turned away just as the tears rolled down my cheeks.

"So, no to the dance. Got it," I murmured hurriedly as I made my way toward the door.

"Wait," he softly called after me.

Icy fingers caught my hand. His body pressed up behind me, and his frosty breath caressed my neck. "I'm sorry," he said. "I want to go. I want to be with you. I want to walk through these halls hand in hand so everyone knows, but we can't. It's not safe. I'm sorry."

He was so close. More tears ran down my cheeks as I closed my eyes to take a deep breath of his fresh, wintry scent, not knowing if it would be for the last time.

"Please, don't cry," Fannar whispered.

"I'm trying," I answered.

Fannar placed his hands on my shoulders and slowly eased me into turning to face him. Before I could do anything else, he leaned down and softly brushed his lips over mine. It was the slightest kiss, but it said everything it needed to. He rested his forehead against mine.

"Enjoy your dance, okay?" he whispered.

I nodded. I broke away from him and hurried out the door, through the library, and back to my dorm room as fast as I could. I flung myself on the bed and sobbed into my pillow.

CHAPTER TEN

Iris stood in front of the mirror that hung on the back of her closet door, admiring her gorgeous knee-length lilac dress. The strapless design was tasteful and elegant with a sweetheart neckline, a sequined bodice, and a slight train that draped gracefully behind her. She had paired the dress with a pair of simple silver-colored pumps, as well as a beautiful silver necklace and matching earrings. She looked at me worriedly.

"Do I look okay?" she asked.

"You look *amazing,* Iris. Stop panicking." I reassured her.

Iris smiled at me. "Thanks, Helena. You do, too!"

I picked a dress that matched my eyes. The floor-length emerald-green satin gave off a regal sheen. The delicate spaghetti straps gracefully draped around my shoulders and back, and the dress hugged my body in all the right places, highlighting my curves. I paired it with gold-colored heels embellished with sparkling rhinestones that glimmered in the light, as well as a single golden bracelet that wrapped around my arm gracefully. Iris was nice enough to style my hair into a sleek and stylish updo. A few curls framed my face next to my dangling rhinestone earrings.

Iris's smile suddenly turned sad. "I'm sorry Fannar said no to the dance, Helena. I can't believe no one asked you to go with them instead. I'm glad you're still going, anyway."

I smiled at that one. I hadn't told her, but *many* guys had asked me to the dance. I just couldn't bring myself to go with anyone other than Fannar.

Instead, I answered, "We should go. It's almost time to meet Guiden."

I didn't have a date, but it was still fun to see Iris with hers. Guiden wore a charcoal gray suit that was perfectly tailored for his large, muscular build—a common trait among Earth Enchanted guys. His black hair was cut short and swept to the side, and his warm brown eyes sparkled whenever he looked at Iris. She went stiff as a board when she saw him.

I nudged her forward. "Hey, Guiden!" I cheered as I pushed the two lovebirds together.

"Hey, Helena," he replied with a nervous smile.

Then he looked at Iris. He blushed and his jaw dropped.

"Iris . . . oh, gods . . . you look . . ."

He trailed off. I could see Iris getting anxious.

"Pretty?" I suggested.

"Beautiful!" he countered.

Iris smiled, blushing a deep red. Guiden offered his arm, and she took it. All three of us walked toward the gym, music booming out from its closed double doors.

When we pushed them open, we were hit with a huge wave of lively music. The gym's high ceiling was strewn with streamers in shades of pink, red, and purple. Balloons scattered across the floor and floated through the air, adding a fun, youthful vibe to the atmosphere. Students made a point to kick the balloons every so often. Snacks and drinks were available in the back of the gym, and round tables and chairs lined the sides. The dance floor was in the middle of the room, with a disco ball spinning and sparkling above it. At the front of the gym was a stage, where Frankie the chef gremlin was at the DJ booth, and colored lights filled the room.

"You . . . care to dance?" Guiden asked Iris.

Iris began to smile, then looked at me worriedly.

"Go dance," I encouraged her.

She put a hand on my arm. "We'll be right back."

Then she took Guiden's hand and walked onto the dance floor. As I watched them leave, I dropped the facade a little and sank. I was happy for them, but . . . I wished Fannar was there. Someone cleared their throat nearby.

"You wanna dance, Drake?"

It was a guy from the Earth Guild. I hadn't seen him before, but he was cute.

I shrugged. "Sure. Why not?" It wasn't like I had anyone else to dance with.

After a while, I'd danced with just about every guy who didn't have a date and even a few who did. It was fun, but not really the most fulfilling. I kept looking at Iris and Guiden, who popped back every now and again to make sure I was okay. Their romance was blossoming before my eyes, from shyly dancing a foot away from each other, to holding hands as they both meekly pranced, to slow dancing with her head on his shoulder.

God, I wish that were me and Fannar . . .

Halfway through the dance, I'd kind of grown tired of all the random guys, and I had to hide just to take a break from all the dancing. I was wondering if it was too early to leave and plotting my exit when Guiden wandered up to me.

"Hey, Guiden," I said pre-emptively. "I'm fine! Tell Iris to stop worrying about me."

He gave me a big goofy grin. "You're going to be even better when you hear this!"

"What?"

"*Guess who's here?*" he said in a sing-song voice.

"Fannar?!" I was almost afraid to say his name and be disappointed.

"Yes! He just walked in!"

I stood from my table and looked around.

"Over there!" Guiden pointed to the side of the gym close to the entrance.

I squinted, searching among all the heaving bodies, moving in time with the music. I only saw him for a second, but I caught his eye.

"Thanks, Guiden!" I said quickly.

"*Go to him!*" Guiden urged dramatically, as if we were in a movie.

I laughed, and my heart began to race as I pushed through the crowd of dancers. Fannar was coming toward me as well. I weaved through the sea of people, determined to fight my way to him until we were finally within arm's reach of each other in the middle of the dance floor.

For a moment, time seemed to stand still. My heart quickened, and I was breathless, captured by his beautiful eyes. I had never seen him so dressed up before, wearing a dark gray suit with a blue tie and his white hair slicked back just a tiny bit. He was the most handsome man I had ever seen. All the noise seemed to fade away as the music shifted into a slow and romantic love song.

Without a word, Fannar's hand touched my elbow and pulled me into his arms. He leaned his forehead against mine and stared into my soul, our bodies swaying to the music. With one glance, all of my longing for Fannar was answered.

"You look beautiful," Fannar said. He touched one of my curls, and the back of his fingers brushed my cheek.

"You came," I whispered with the biggest smile. "What changed your mind?"

"If not now, then when?" He smiled back affectionately.

I wasn't exactly sure what he meant, but this wasn't the time to question him. I was in his arms, and I was going to savor every moment. As I leaned in closer, my body lightly pressed against his. His arms, chest, hips, legs—all touching mine in a captivating embrace. Cold radiated through his clothes, and his heart was beating as fast as mine was.

I rested my head on his shoulder and closed my eyes. It was just Fannar and me at that moment. The world around us seemed to disappear, and the two of us were all there was.

As we continued to sway to the melody, the music swelled, and I knew the song would be over soon. I leaned back so I could get lost in his arctic-blue eyes again. I was in a dream and never wanted it to end.

As the last notes of the song faded into the air, he looked at my lips. *Will he kiss me in front of everyone?*

"Hey, Drake! Come dance with me!" a loud voice interjected.

A blazing hot hand grabbed my arm. I recoiled, yanking my arm out of the burning grip, turning away from Fannar to see who I needed to murder for interrupting our moment. It was a Fire Enchanted that I recalled dancing with earlier, but it wasn't all that memorable.

"Excuse me!" I snapped at him. "I already danced with you."

"Come on, one more dance! Iceman had his turn!" He grabbed my arm again.

"Let go of me!"

He started scowling. "What's your problem? Think you're too good for me, Drake?!"

"I said, LET GO!" I clenched my fists, and my powers flared as I pulled away from him again.

Before I could do anything, the air chilled around us. The Fire douche yelped and grabbed his legs. They were frozen to the ground, all the way to his calves. In an instant, Fannar had him by the collar and got in his face.

"Listen here, you piece of shit," Fannar snarled at him. "When a lady tells you to let her go, you *do it*." His brow furrowed even more intensely with anger. "Especially when she's *my* lady!"

"O-*okay!*"

"I mean it," Fannar growled just quietly enough so that we could hear. "Touch her one more time, and I'll freeze your legs again and shatter them at the knees."

Fannar gave the Fire Enchanted a harsh shove, and the ice around his legs broke. Suddenly free, the guy stumbled backward and fell on his butt.

By then, one of the chaperones saw something was happening and began making his way through the crowded dance floor toward us.

"Let's go!" Fannar said, and his familiar cold fingers grasped my hand.

As he led me through the crowd, I looked back at Fire douche on his ass and giggled as we continued to flee. Once we exited the gym, Fannar was laughing as well. It was the first time that I heard him really laugh, and the realization was bittersweet because it had taken so long.

He continued leading me at a brisk pace.

"Where are we going?" I asked.

"My room," he answered.

When we got into his dorm room, Fannar shut the door and sighed. "No way anyone followed us this far!"

His dorm room was the same size as the one I shared with Iris, but he didn't have any of the standard-issue academy dorm furniture. Instead, the entire room had an airy, modern atmosphere. His desk was a white marble table with shiny metal legs, paired with a sleek chrome swivel chair with a bright blue back and cushion.

The walls were decorated with abstract artwork in various shades of blue on white backgrounds, adding a hint of sophistication to the space. A tapestry on one wall stood out and almost felt out of place among the abstract and contemporary decor. It looked old and featured a beautiful frozen landscape with a castle in the center. The bed was also a mix of sleek, modern lines and comfortable curves, with an eye-catching blue and white comforter and more pillows than I'd ever seen in one place.

"You don't have a roommate?" I said, observing only one set of furniture.

"No," he answered. "My parents didn't want me to have a roommate that wasn't Ice Enchanted, and Headmaster Moira said she couldn't accommodate that kind of request. So they paid extra for a private room to keep me away from any potential non-Ice Enchanted friends."

"Oh, the irony!" I gave him a coy smirk but quickly took a more serious tone. "So, tell me, what did you mean when you said, 'If not now, then when'?"

He wandered over to his bed and sat down. I sat next to him.

"If I don't stand up to my parents now, when will I ever?" He stared at the floor as he spoke. "They decide everything in my life without ever asking me what I want. They just say, 'This is what a prince should do. This is how a prince should act.' I didn't even have the balls to keep them from marrying off Gwyneira, not really." Fannar turned abruptly and looked deep into my eyes. "But when I saw you leave after you had so sweetly asked me to the dance . . . I wondered if that would be the last time I was ever going to be close to you. I just couldn't let it happen. If I let you walk away for good, Helena, I'd never forgive myself."

I started getting teary-eyed again. Fannar took my hand.

"I'm not going to live in fear of them," he continued. "If they find out, whatever they try to do, I'll protect you. I promise."

"Thanks," I smirked. "But you know I do a pretty good job of protecting myself, so maybe I'll protect *you*!"

"Fine." Fannar smiled. "We'll protect each other."

He reached out and cupped my face in one hand, staring so deeply into my eyes, like he was reading my soul. His lips brushed mine softly before he pressed them into the most gentle, tender kiss, blanketing me in comfort before looking at me again.

"You know, back there," I said coyly, "You called me 'your lady.'"

He gave me a sly smile. "You are."

He sensuously ran his thumb over the back of my hand, knowing it would send ripples of icy sensation through my body. I gasped quietly, shivering from his touch. He smiled devilishly and leaned in.

This time, it wasn't a light, gentle kiss, but a deep one, a kiss that eased my mouth open and let his cold tongue claim me with a fierce passion. Slowly, he caressed the inside of my mouth, our tongues embracing each other.

He slowly unzipped the back of my dress with torturous care. His fingers grazed over my skin as he delicately slipped the dress off my shoulders, revealing my bare breasts to the cool air of the room. My panties followed suit, sliding down my legs with ease. He gently lowered me onto the soft bed sheets, his hands caressing every inch of my bare skin as he positioned me comfortably on the bed. As I my warm body rested against the cool sheets, a shiver ran through me and my nipples hardened in response.

He towered over me as I lay naked in his bed, his eyes slowly gazing over me.

"I've never seen anything so beautiful," he said softly.

He leaned down and kissed me again in another long, deep kiss. His hands glided over my chest, sending tingles through me as they explored. He gazed down at me with a hunger in his eyes. When he reached my breasts, he gently took them into his hands. His fingers moved tenderly, exploring their roundness before his lips brushed against them. I whimpered as his mouth slowly descended on one, kissing the creamy curves of its contour, before enveloping my sensitive nipple, sucking lightly as his tongue teased and circled it. His tongue licked and teased each nipple as he suckled softly, steadily increasing the intensity until I was gasping for breath beneath him.

He slowly savored each breast as he moved from one to the other, leaving a whisper of coolness and a trail of goosebumps in their wake. His movements were unhurried and filled with desire, every press of his lips sending sparks of pleasure through my body.

He leaned back and took off his shirt. I enjoyed the view of his bare chest, so perfectly shaped. His hands moved down to his pants, and as he began unbuckling his belt, my hands roamed his chest. The feeling of his abs under my fingers sent a shudder of pleasure through me already—even more when he moaned by my ear. *"Oh, you're so warm . . ."*

Once his clothes were off, his arms wound around me, pulling me into him. As my naked body pressed against his bare skin for the first time, I gasped helplessly in pleasure.

His skin was so soft, and it was so cold on mine that it was like a static shock when he first touched me. But it was soon an appetizing chill, like a cold shower when it was too hot outside.

Fannar moaned softly again as he pulled me close. His lips moved down to claim my mouth again. Then he leaned to my ear, kissed my neck a few times, then whispered. "You're so hot . . . Can I feel how hot you are when I'm inside you?"

My body shuddered in delight at his whispered words. "Yes," I gasped.

He kissed me again, leaning me down. His fingers began to trail down my body, starting from my neck, over my breasts, across my stomach, to the inside of my thigh, and pressed on my legs, easing them open. As his fingers slipped between my folds, curling them upward, the shudder of cold from his hand sent such a shockwave through me that I cried out. Fannar gave a deep, throaty chuckle. My back arched as the slow, gentle, delicious movements of his fingers sent pulses of pleasure through me.

Soon, his fingers pulled away, and I gasped as his tip pressed against me. He slowly moved inside, softly moaning as he did. I shuddered helplessly as he slipped in deeper, inch by delicious inch, his fervent kisses swallowing my cries of pleasure, until the entire icy length of his arousal pressed deep inside my fluttering core.

He's so cold!

The cold sent shivers of all kinds up my body, spreading goosebumps over the surface of my skin. Every inch of him inside me was pure ecstasy—the feeling of being filled with him was incomparable. He moved slowly at first, each drag out and thrust in adding to the pulse of rapture coursing through me.

His hands roamed my body, exploring every inch of me as we moved together, squeezing and caressing my curves. His gaze burned with desire and hunger as he leaned into me. He was powerful and confident, pushing and pulling in perfect rhythm, taking me to the edge of pleasure.

His lips found mine as he thrust into me deeply. Our mouths clashed in a passionate embrace as he increased the speed of his thrusts, pushing deeper with each one. My head fell backward, and more moans escaped me.

Fannar's chest rested on mine, and I felt the cold radiating from him, his hammering heart, his moans in my ear. I could smell him, the smell of freshly fallen snow, and felt his arctic breath fanning out over my neck.

It was a beautiful clash—his cold and my warmth. His breath, his skin, even his smell was all *so* wintery. My body seemed to recognize its cold and fight it—heating me more and more in response to his very being.

His hard and urgent thrusts sent shockwaves through my body. As I raked my hands through his hair and clawed my nails down his back, he moaned loudly.

"Yes! Like that! Harder!" he urged.

My nails dug into his back as I pulled at him even more. All I could see, all I could smell, all I could feel was him. I felt contained and safe with him. Pleasure built in my core, and I could tell Fannar felt it too—every muscle in his body began to tense up as he accelerated his thrusts and his moans increased. Faster, stronger, the passion piled up, frothing and boiling inside my body—I couldn't take it anymore.

A sparkling wave of pleasure exploded through my body, and I tried to muffle my screams. My back arched in bliss. Stuttering, whimpering, I clutched his back. He moaned in my ear, his sensuous thrusts within my still quivering core promising me he would not stop until he was completely satisfied, too.

Fannar's hands clamped down on me like a vice. His breath came in quick, jagged gasps as he rocked back and forth inside of me, grunting with exertion. He let out a roar of triumph as he emptied himself into me in one uncontainable burst, and the icy warmth of his release flooded through me.

When it was over, he toppled breathlessly next to me on the bed. As I caught my own breath, Fannar spooned me, pulling me into him. He felt so much warmer . . . or perhaps I was cooler. Or maybe it was both, our elements blending together as we were united.

He kissed my cheek. "I love you, Helena."

"I love you, too, Fannar."

He pulled me in tighter, his strong, icy arms closing around me. I had never felt so safe as when I was in his arms, like nothing could ever hurt me. Sleep soon came.

CHAPTER ELEVEN

I didn't know why they called it the walk of shame. Although I had to sneak out of Fannar's room before sunrise so people didn't spot me leaving his room, I was striding through the halls with pride and a skip in my step. When I reached my dorm, I knocked on the door in case Iris had had a wild night as well. Shuffling and muffled voices immediately followed.

"It's okay," I called in. "It's just me."

The shuffling calmed down a bit, and then Iris opened the door with a shy smile.

"Oh, Helena! Come in, quick!"

When I hustled in, Guiden fixed his disheveled pants and pulled a shirt over his bedhead.

"Guiden, hurry and get out of here before we all get in trouble!"

"We know!" Iris giggled. "He's leaving!"

They both started laughing like school children, then shared a little kiss before Guiden snuck out of the room.

Once Iris closed the door, I cocked an eyebrow at her. She caught my eye and broke out into sheepish laughter.

"I'm guessing it went well?" I asked.

"I don't kiss and tell!" Iris squeaked before looking over at me. "Were you with Fannar last night?"

"I was."

Iris smiled at me and flopped back on her bed. "I'm happy for you guys."

"I'm happy for you guys, too."

Iris fell back asleep as I quickly changed out of my dress to catch a few more hours of sleep.

We wound up sleeping in that morning, skipping breakfast, and headed to the cafeteria for an early lunch. Once we got to the front of the line, even Frankie still looked like he was hungover.

"Hey, Frankie," Iris said.

He gave a grunting warble, flapping a hand.

"Chef's salad, please," Iris requested.

He conjured up the salad, then rubbed his yellow eyes with a red thumb and forefinger.

"Good morning. Can I have a ham and cheese sandwich?" I asked.

Frankie nodded, then summoned my order for me. I picked it up, but before I left, I said. "Hey, Frankie. Great music last night!"

The little gremlin finally gave me a genuine smile.

Yes! He likes me! Finally!

Once we entered the dining area to sit down, a disturbing silence rang out. Iris looked around anxiously as the silence took hold. I was scared to look around, but when I did, I saw all eyes on me. My heart sank to the bottom of my shoes.

Oh, crap.

"Why are they staring at you?" Iris whispered to me as we quickly picked a table. "Do you think it's because of Fannar?"

"What else would it be?" I muttered.

"This looks really bad."

"Yeah, I need to find Fannar and see if he knows what's going on. This is way worse than last time there were just rumors about us."

"Yeah, let's eat fast and get out of here."

Under the watchful eyes of everyone there, Iris and I ate at record speed. We hurried out of the cafeteria to Fannar's room. Fannar let us in. Guiden was there, too.

"Everyone was staring at Helena during lunch!" Iris recounted to the others.

"I heard what was going on when I went to breakfast this morning and came to look for Fannar right away," Guiden said. He cringed and looked up at me. "Helena, do you remember that one guy you shoved away at the dance?"

"Yeah, that Fire douchebag," I answered. "What about him?"

"Turns out that was the son of a Fire lord," Fannar explained. "And a liar on top of that."

I scowled. "Did you know he's a lord?"

"No, the academy tries not to emphasize titles and status here," Guiden explained. "That's why no one ever addresses Fannar as Prince or Your Royal Highness like we would in the kingdoms. I don't even know who the lords from the Earth Guild are."

"What did the guy lie about?" Iris asked nervously.

Fannar had his ice mask back on, as well as a cold and emotionless voice.

That's gotta be a bad sign.

"He told his father that you were his girlfriend, and I stole you from him," Fannar said, anger flickering over his glassy eyes. "Then I threatened his life."

"What?!" I snapped.

"That's not all," he continued. "His father was *pissed* and apparently reported my behavior to the Fire Council, which governs the Fire Kingdom. Coveting something of the other kingdom's is a serious offense."

"*'Coveting something'*?" I repeated, infuriated. "What am I, a vase? I can't be coveted!"

"Since Fannar is the Ice Prince," Guiden began, "the rumor is that the Fire Council is taking this as an intentionally hostile act by the Ice Kingdom. This could lead to war between the Fire and Ice Kingdoms."

"Are you serious?" I asked. "Fannar intervened when some asshole couldn't take no for an answer, and now there might be a full-blown war?! This is insane."

Fannar sighed. "There's also no telling how my parents will react if they hear that the Fire Kingdom is thinking about declaring war," he thought out loud, scowling in resentful silence. "They might pre-emptively attack just to make a statement."

"So what can we do?" Iris asked.

"Fannar and I talked about it," Guiden said, "and we think . . . Maybe you should say it, Fannar."

Fannar took my hand and gave me a sad but thoughtful look.

"We think it would be best if you and I stayed away from each other for a while," he told me.

My body instantly stiffened, and Iris looked at me with concern.

"Just until this blows over," he continued.

"What do you mean?" I asked, my voice quivering a little. "You don't want to see me anymore?"

"No, of course not." Fannar shook his head.

"It's obvious that that douchebag started all this because of his pride," Guiden offered. "If you guys aren't together, then he won't be constantly reminded of your rejection and have an excuse to try to start a war between both kingdoms. With a little time, I'm sure he'll move on to something else, and everything will just blow over. We just can't let that Fire asshole manipulate everyone into starting a war over his fragile ego."

"But they just finally got together!" Iris protested.

Guiden saw that my eyes began to fill with tears.

"Iris," Guiden pulled Iris toward the door. "Let's give them a moment."

Iris looked at me with worry.

I nodded at her.

"We'll be outside," she said softly, and they closed the door behind them.

My throat tightened, and my heart started racing. "Last night, you said we would fight for us, Fannar!" I blurted abruptly.

"I meant my parents," he responded. "We're talking about war now. People could die. Shouldn't we do whatever we can to prevent war from breaking out between our kingdoms? Right now, this seems to be the best option."

"But I don't want to be away from you." Tears rolled down my cheeks.

He pulled me into his arms. "I know, and I don't want to be away from you either. It's only temporary. Once this blows over, we can be together again."

"Why can't we just meet in secret or something?"

"It's too risky. You shouldn't even be in my room right now. You know how fast gossip spreads here. We don't know who will talk to whom. I can't put my people in jeopardy."

My stomach dropped. I pulled away from him. "What do you mean?" I demanded.

Fannar frowned. "I have a duty to my people," he said firmly. "I'm their future king. I cannot endanger the Ice Kingdom unnecessarily."

I felt my anger flare up. "Unnecessarily?" I asked. "I'm unnecessary?!"

"That's not what I meant!"

Is he saying that his duty is more important than me? More important than our love for each other?

"What about us?" I asked. "Shouldn't our love overcome anything?"

"It's not that simple, Helena," he sighed. "This isn't a fairy tale. I have to do my best to maintain what peace we have left with the Fire Kingdom."

I looked away, biting my lip. Logically, I knew he was right, but my broken heart still felt betrayed. We had finally come together, only to be torn apart again by some jerk. We should flaunt our relationship to prove that nobody could keep us apart—not even him. I wanted to scream and cry, to rail against the unfairness of it all.

"I feel like I've been cheated!" I yelled with frustration. "It took me so long to get you to go against your parents and be with me. Now, this happens!"

"It's not about you!" he shot back. "You don't understand because you're not from here." His bitterly frosty glare was back, and he crossed his arms in front of his chest. "You can be so stubborn. Typical Fire Enchanted."

I gasped loudly from the shock of his words. Anger began to flood my chest. I wanted to slap him for insulting me, but all I could muster was pinning him with a deadly glare. We stood in stony silence. The tension was heavy as an invisible wall formed between us. "Forget it," I snarled and wiped my eyes. "You don't have to worry about us staying away from each other. It's over."

Without letting Fannar utter another word, I rushed out, throwing the door open with a loud bang, and flounced past Iris and Guiden.

"Helena?" Iris called after me.

I didn't stop. She ran to catch up with me and linked her arm with mine as we walked back to our room.

I sobbed uncontrollably in her arms. Sadness overwhelmed me. The tears wouldn't stop, and neither would the hurt that had taken up residence in my heart, where my dreams of Fannar used to be.

CHAPTER TWELVE

I often fell asleep reliving the night of the dance, only to wake up in the middle of the night with my heart heavy with misery. The memories of the day that Fannar and I broke up still haunted me. I'd stare at the ceiling, replaying our argument in my head, my words, his words, and the deep sorrow in my chest that no amount of tears could wash away.

The morning after our argument, my conscience crept in. I wasn't selfish enough to expect Fannar to prioritize me over his kingdom. I understood that our actions could potentially put two kingdoms in danger, and I couldn't live with myself if people died because our relationship started a war. Fannar was right. He had a duty to his people as their future king. It should have been an obvious decision for me, too, but it was still ridiculously difficult to come to terms with it. But I wasn't willing to admit that to Fannar, not after what he said about not being from the Enchanted Realm and calling me a "typical Fire Enchanted."

It was now the first week of November, two weeks since we had broken up, two weeks since I had seen him. Too afraid of the hurt I'd feel if I saw him face-to-face, I started taking longer routes to classes and avoiding all the places he hung out. My plan seemed to be working, but it was a struggle every single day. As much as I wanted to forget him and move on with my life, a larger part of me still held onto him. But as each day passed, it got easier to continue despite the pain.

To keep my mind off him, I threw myself into my studies and training, using them as fuel to keep pushing forward. I blocked out the whispers of my classmates. I put on a brave face in class, determined not to let my broken heart show. I told myself that one day things would get better, my heart would mend, and it wouldn't be as painful anymore.

On Thursday before class, I had to drop off some paperwork at the Administration Office. I had to skip breakfast with Iris, but it felt good to break out of my routine.

The walk was so pretty that time of the morning. A light chill filled the air as the sun's rays were just beginning to break through patches of gray clouds. Droplets of dew glistened in the soft morning light on the blades of grass and leaves. A bird chirped occasionally to beckon the sun further from its hiding place.

As I walked along the path, I approached the library. Ahead was a group of people gathered under a tree, several of them with silver hair glinting in the light.

Dammit! Ice Enchanted.

There was no way I could avoid walking past. I prayed Fannar wasn't with them.

But, of course, he was. He hadn't noticed me yet, so I stole a few moments to glance at him. *So gorgeous.* He stood tall and confident. His snowy hair flowed softly in the breeze, emphasizing his strong, angular jawline and aquamarine eyes that sparkled in the morning sun. His expression was focused and intense as he talked with his friends, his mouth occasionally turning upward in a small smirk.

He turned his head and our eyes met. In an instant, my heart stopped and my breath caught with overwhelming longing for him. But it was quickly replaced by a deep sadness, and I averted my gaze, not wanting to see his face again. I hastened my pace, not looking back as I walked past his group.

That night, Iris and I were about to head out to the cafeteria for dinner when a strong, familiar knock rapped on our door.

"Hi, hon," Iris greeted Guiden and let him into the room. "We were about to go to dinner. You want to join us?"

"Sure," he replied. "But I need to tell you both something first. Ummm . . . Helena, you should sit down. This is a doozy."

I gave Iris a worried look, and I sat down on my bed.

"What is it?" Iris urged.

"I started asking around about Cid Farias," Guiden began.

"Who?" I asked.

"Cid Farias," Guiden repeated. "Fire douchebag. That's his name."

"Oh, Fire douche," Iris nodded.

"Well, I started asking some buddies of mine in the Fire Guild about him and how he reported Fannar to his father," Guiden continued. "None of them knew what I was talking about, but they said he had a history of exaggerating things. I got more suspicious because we're all worried about this guy starting a potential war between the Fire and Ice Kingdoms. I have a friend who is interning for one of the members of the Fire Council this year, so I asked him if he had heard anything about Fannar attacking Cid and it causing a rift between the kingdoms. He just got back to me. He hasn't heard a thing, not about Fannar, and he's never even heard of Cid or Helena, for that matter. All this crap we were worried about was over nothing."

"What?!" Iris exclaimed.

Guiden shook his head. "I had one of my Fire buddies ask Cid directly. Cid never even told his father. They were just rumors that got blown out of proportion."

"That's wonderful!" Iris said excitedly.

I looked down at my hands folded in my lap, trying to process everything Guiden just said.

"Yes!" Guiden agreed and looked at me. "That means that you and Fannar have no reason to be separated anymore!"

"You guys can be together!" Iris's smile fell when she saw my less-than-happy expression. "Helena?"

"Does he know?" I asked, still not looking away from my hands.

"No," Guiden answered. "I'm going to tell him if I see him at dinner or find him after."

I bit my lip. Our fight was about nothing. None of us bothered to verify the rumors before talking about a separation. But words were said that I couldn't forget.

"I'm glad there's no risk of war," I began, "but this doesn't change anything between me and Fannar. I haven't forgiven him for what he said."

"It was the heat of the moment," Guiden reasoned. "We all know he cares about you."

"Guiden is right," Iris agreed. "The two of you should at least talk things out."

"I'm not ready yet," I huffed.

"Guiden"—Iris looked at him—"why don't you give me a few minutes with Helena?"

"Sure," he responded. "I'll see you in the cafeteria in a bit." He left the room.

Iris gave me a stern look.

"What?" I asked with a little attitude.

"Helena," she began, "you know Fannar is a prince. He has a responsibility to his kingdom that he can't just put aside for you. I think you were asking for too much."

"I know," I conceded. "You're right. I don't want to put him in a position where he has to choose between his duty and me. I never meant to do that. I guess I just wanted him to reassure me that he loved me and that we could get through anything together. I know I was being difficult, but, at that moment, that's how I felt."

"You have to trust that he loves you and respects you enough to do the best he can for your relationship, but his first priority is going to be to his people."

"I know." I sighed.

"Don't you think you owe him an apology then?"

"Maybe . . . but he owes me one, too! He told me I wouldn't understand because of where I'm from and called me a stubborn Fire Enchanted."

"Wasn't that how you were acting?" Iris asked slyly.

I scowled. "It was insulting."

"You're being stubborn right now. I obviously can't force you to do anything, but you've been miserable since you guys broke up, and now you have a chance to be together again. I hope you at least try to talk to him."

"I'll think about it, but don't hold your breath."

"Fine, let's go to dinner."

"Iris?" I stopped her before we headed out the door. "Thanks for being here for me. I really appreciate it."

I hugged her.

"Of course!" She smiled. "We're sisters from another mister! We may not always agree, but I still love ya!"

The following Monday, as I was on my way to class, Guiden walked toward me, his backpack slung over his shoulder. When he saw me, he waved me down and bounded over with enthusiasm.

"Hey, Helena!" he called.

"Hi, Guiden!" I responded and stopped to chat.

"Good thing I caught you. I saw Fannar this morning."

A sudden surge of emotion stunned me as soon as I heard Fannar's name. I tried to keep my composure, masking my inner turmoil, but my insides churned with a maelstrom of sadness and anxiety in anticipation of what Guiden had to say.

"And he said that you borrowed some history notes from him?" Guiden asked.

"Yeah, I did." I nodded.

"He said he needs them back."

"Why doesn't he ask me himself?" I scowled slightly.

"He knows you're avoiding him on purpose."

Well, I couldn't deny that.

"Okay," I said. "They're in my room. I can give them to you tonight to give to him."

"Sorry, I can't. I have a meeting tonight. Just give them back yourself."

"But—"

"C'mon, stop acting like a bunch of high schoolers," he half-joked as he turned away to leave. "You can't avoid him for the next two years. Just talk to him."

Guiden walked away before I could argue any further.

CHAPTER THIRTEEN

I stood in front of Fannar's private study room at the library, feeling an unfamiliar mix of emotions. Nervousness and anticipation seemed to be the strongest, but there was a hint of sorrow and resignation as well. I hadn't been there since we'd broken up, and the memories it brought back were both sweet and heart-wrenching.

The library was mostly dark, with just a few lights on so the last stragglers could get around. I had waited until after dinner to come, spending most of the afternoon trying to prepare myself for this moment.

The light from the table lamp glowed through the slit under the door, so I knew he was probably inside. I took a deep breath and knocked. There was shuffling from inside before the door swung open.

With a swift glance, I recognized Fannar in the doorway, but I forced myself to turn away. I refused to let my gaze linger on his face for more than a moment, knowing the raw emotion that would surface if I did.

"I have your notes," I stated flatly as I slipped a backpack strap off one shoulder and flipped the bag in front of me so I could unzip it.

I fumbled with the zipper nervously. It was caught, so I tugged it harder, dropping my backpack on the ground.

I quickly bent down to pick it up, but so did Fannar. We both reached for it at the same time, and our hands brushed. A wonderful cooling sensation rushed through me, but I recoiled immediately, not wanting to get lost in it.

"Just come in," he said, grabbing hold of my bag and walking back into the study room with it.

I followed him into the room, the door locking behind me. He set my bag on the table, and I silently rummaged through it until I found his notebook.

"Here," I held out the notebook, still not looking at him, averting my gaze to the carpet to his right instead.

After he took it from me, I quickly turned to get to my backpack and leave, but his hand grabbed one of mine.

"Wait," he said. "Look at me."

I shook my head.

His fingers touched my chin and tilted my head up to face him. His glacial blue eyes locked on mine. I had forgotten how good his touch felt and how passionate his gaze was. The comforting familiarity of it brought a flood of visceral emotions, and the sheer weight of how much I'd missed him collapsed on me. Tears began to well up.

"No, don't cry," he whispered, leaning into me.

I closed my eyes as his lips softly brushed against mine before kissing me gently, lingering as if he never wanted the moment to end.

When his lips pulled away, he opened his arms to wrap me in a tight embrace. My body pressed against his. His face was so close that I could feel his breath on my cheek and take in his wintry scent. His bright blue eyes brimmed with tenderness and longing.

"I missed you," he said.

Guilt and regret overwhelmed me.

"I'm so sorry, Fannar," I apologized as a tear ran down my face. "I never wanted you to choose between me and your people. I was just upset. I know protecting your kingdom comes first. It *should* come first."

"I should have tried harder to find another way before suggesting that we separate," he admitted, stroking my cheek. "And we should have looked into the rumors before doing anything."

"We talk first before making rash decisions, okay?" I asked.

He nodded and continued. "I'm sorry about what I said. It's because you're not from the Enchanted Realm that makes you so special. You bring something different here that no one else can."

"You also called me a 'stubborn Fire Enchanted,'" I pouted.

"That part is true," he chuckled, his eyes sparkling. He cupped my cheeks in his palms and smiled at me. "But that's why I fell in love with you. Who else but a stubborn Fire Enchanted could do this to me?"

Who would've ever thought that being called stubborn would be so romantic? I gazed into Fannar's icy blue eyes, and my heart swelled.

"I love you," I said.

"I love you, too," he responded.

Fannar caressed my face tenderly and leaned in to kiss me again. This time it was passionate, full of the love and desire we'd been repressing since we'd broken up. His lips moved against mine with an urgency that showed how much he had missed me, too.

The fire of passion ignited within me. I ravished his mouth, my tongue hungrily sliding against his. His moan reverberated around us as I tasted every corner of his mouth, reveling in the deliciousness of his kiss. My tongue moved feverishly, our desire for one another seeming to build with every passing second.

Our bodies pressed together and began to intertwine, begging to become one. His kisses trailed from my lips down to my neck as his hand slowly cupped my breast over my shirt.

As I took a breath, I whispered, "I want you right now."

Fannar leaned back to look at me. "Here?" he asked breathlessly.

I nodded with a sly smile, leaning my backside against the table.

His lips returned to mine, and his cold hands dipped into the collar of my blazer, unbuttoning my shirt. He was more forceful this time, more determined and certain, like he had lost his reserve during our dry spell. He knew what he wanted, and he wasn't shy about it.

His icy hands slipped over my shoulders and eased the clothes off my body. His frosty fingers slipped under and unhooked my bra. As he slid it off me impatiently, I could feel myself already arching into his touch.

The chill he left over my body made my skin ripple in goosebumps—and my nipples harden. He looked at them and gave a low, throaty chuckle. Those wicked, arctic eyes fixed on my face as his cold hands gently caressed my breasts and traced circles around each sensitive peak. The pleasure sparked through my chest, taking my breath away, before dancing between my legs.

A soft moan escaped me, and Fannar gave another aroused chuckle. His fingers ran around the tips of my breasts over and over again. The sensation was so intense that the pleasure almost bordered on pain. Every little touch of his fingers sent a small pulse of arousal shuddering through my body. I whimpered, my tone getting weaker and weaker in breathlessness as he touched me.

He leaned close to my ear. "I love that sound you make."

I couldn't speak. I could barely breathe. I gave a little pleasured whine and tightly gripped his shoulder to show him what he was doing to me.

His head ducked down, and, for a moment, he stopped. As his fingers were replaced with his tongue, a bolt of sensation made me cry out. His tongue lightly pressed on my nipple—as cold and as wet as a melting ice cube on my breast—and then lavished a slow, deep lick with his whole tongue before dragging it across both breasts. I gripped the edge of the table with my hands as my back arched and my chest begged for more. The *cold,* the *wet,* every little tingle as his tongue moved across me—I could barely take it.

"Fannar . . ." I moaned.

His tongue shifted into a point and flicked my erect nipple in a frenzied, torturous dance, sending shockwaves of pleasure and pain that spread through my body like wildfire. The cold increased the pleasure tenfold. His relentless lapping built up to an almost unbearable intensity. I moaned as he ravished me with his tongue.

Fannar lifted his head and pressed his body closer to me. His solid member was pressing against my thigh, and when his chest met mine, he whispered in my ear. "Can we try something?"

"What?"

"Can you heat your hands up—I mean *really* heat them up, almost on fire—and . . . touch me?"

I looked at him, arousal pounding my body, and gave him a grin, biting my lip.

"Okay," I murmured.

He leaned back—just enough to give him the space to unbutton his shirt and shrug it off his body, revealing his perfectly sculpted chest and abs.

I clenched my fists, heat coursing through my body. Once my hands were glowing just a little, I reached for him.

His eyes sparkled—in excitement and just a touch of fear—as I placed my overheated hands on his chest.

"Oh, gods!" he groaned immediately on contact.

I lifted my hands off him quickly, concerned that I had burned him, but he looked up at me with a grin.

"I didn't say stop!" he laughed.

I ran my hands up and down his bare chest, enjoying the feel of his rock-hard abs and muscles clenching as he cried out in pleasure under my palms. I felt so powerful. He was completely at my mercy for how much pleasure or pain I wanted to give him. His stiffness pressed against the inside of my thigh and gave me an idea.

I unbuckled his pants, and he stripped them off. As I continued to touch his chest, I dipped my other hand down and clutched his shaft with my heated hand. Fannar jumped and yelped under my sudden grasp. I cupped him in a loose grasp and slowly worked my hand up and down.

He gave a light moan, and his freezing hand gripped my wrist, guiding its motion, starting slow and steadily growing faster. His breathing got heavier, and when he tensed up, I let go.

Fannar's hands slid around my waist, roughly turning me around, and bent me over the table. He reached under my skirt and pulled down my panties, letting them fall to the floor. His body spooned over me, and he grabbed both of my hips.

I gasped when he entered me in one swift motion, every inch of him thrusting deep inside me. At first, my insides flinched at his chilly presence, then wrapped around him in a warm embrace. The sensation was so intense that I had to bite down on my lip to keep myself quiet. As he slowly stroked, his muscular arms wrapped around me, holding me in place, and his hands aggressively prowled over my breasts, kneading them and adding another layer of sheer delight.

Fannar brushed my hair aside so he could get a better view of my face. My moans grew louder as he thrust harder and faster, each swing of his hips growing more urgent. As the pleasure built up inside me, I pushed back against him with each thrust, intensifying the feeling even more. Pleasure tingled as he drew out, then tremored through me as he thrust in again. His moans became deeper, more guttural as he got closer to his own climax while mine was coming up fast.

My body arched as a tidal wave of ecstasy rolled over me in an eternal moment of perfect bliss. My hands gripped the edges of the table for dear life as Fannar continued to pound into me, driving his hips forward with each thrust until he released his pleasure into me with a deep groan that reverberated through the room.

The cold and heat swirled around inside me. All my energy was spent, and I crumpled onto the table with Fannar collapsing beside me. I rolled onto his chest, which heaved in panting breath. His hand ran up and down my back. My leg hitched to his waist, and his arm wrapped around my body. He pulled me further into his chest and kissed the top of my head.

We stayed like that for what felt like forever, not needing to say anything at all, just happy to be back in each other's arms.

CHAPTER FOURTEEN

The whispers were unavoidable. A month had passed since we'd made up, and I was officially his girlfriend. It wasn't surprising that our classmates gawked at us. Fire and ice aren't supposed to mix, right? Let alone the Ice Prince dating the Fire Enchanted from the Unenchanted Realm. Whether Fannar and I were together or not, people would talk, so we didn't let it bother us. Our relationship was on full display to the world.

We didn't have to pretend we disliked each other anymore. As Fannar had wished, we strolled the halls of the academy hand in hand as he walked me to class. His arm draped around my shoulders if we stopped to chat with friends. Our love was visible every time our eyes met, and we didn't care who saw it.

Yes, we were different, opposites even, but we embraced our differences and found greater strength in them.

We fell into a comfortable new routine together, usually meeting up with Iris and Guiden for lunch in the cafeteria and spending the afternoons poring over homework in Fannar's study room.

December was upon us, and, with that, final exams and winter break were just a few weeks away. It was Thursday morning when I heard Dawn and Jimmy's voices while walking through the courtyard.

"Hey, Drake!" Dawn said, her eyes sparkling with excitement. "I was hoping we'd run into you this morning."

"Hey, guys. What's up?" I asked.

"A bunch of us from the Fire Guild are going into town tonight to watch the new *Dragon Blaze* movie. You should come!"

Jimmy nodded eagerly in agreement. "You're *the* drake! You have to come!"

I smiled at their enthusiasm but, as fun as a dragon movie sounded, shook my head. "Thanks for thinking of me, but I already have plans to study with Fannar. Enchanted Realm History is kicking my butt again."

They exchanged a mischievous glance before turning back to me.

"Study, huh?" Jimmy eyed me suspiciously.

Dawn's grin widened as she playfully asked, "How much *studying* are you two really doing?" She gave me a sly look.

My cheeks heated up as Jimmy snickered beside her.

"Stop it!" I laughed awkwardly. "We're really studying!"

Dawn seemed satisfied with that answer, but Jimmy leaned in closer, a glint in his eye. "Sure, sure. Whatever you say, Drake. Just don't melt your prince-y when things get hot."

"You're the worst!" I exclaimed.

"Okay, enough teasing her." Dawn grabbed Jimmy's hand and began to turn away. "If you change your mind, you know where to find us!"

With that, they waved and headed off. Feeling both flustered and amused, I continued on my way through the courtyard.

As usual, I planned to meet up with Fannar in front of the library, where he hung out with his Ice Enchanted buddies. At that point, the majority of his friends had warmed up to me—as much as they could manage, that is.

I stopped in front of their group at a comfortable distance, staying on the pathway.

"Hi, boys," I greeted with a slight wave.

One of them nudged Fannar, and he looked up with concern on his face.

"Drake," Aspen acknowledged.

"I'll catch you guys later," Fannar said as he joined me on the sidewalk, and we began walking toward my first class.

"What's wrong?" I asked.

He sighed. "Aspen went home this weekend," he began. "His parents asked him about us."

"About us?" I repeated.

"Yeah, sounds like everyone in the Ice Kingdom knows."

"Even your parents?"

"Yeah, Aspen's parents and mine are close. That's how it came up."

I let out a deep breath and thought for a moment. I couldn't keep the worry from creeping into my voice as I asked, "And how are they taking it?"

"From what Aspen's parents told him, it doesn't sound good."

"Are they going to try to stop us from being together?"

Fannar shook his head and put his arm around me in a comforting gesture. "We'll just have to wait and see." He shrugged. "It doesn't matter. We knew this was going to happen, and we're not going to put our relationship on pause for them. They can't do anything to us as long as we're at the academy." He attempted to flash a reassuring smile, but there was still an underlying tension in his voice.

I nodded and leaned my head on his shoulder. "Whatever happens, we'll figure it out."

An alarm started wailing, waking me up from my deep slumber. The early morning light streamed through the window. After studying, I had spent the night in Fannar's room, and he immediately jumped out of bed. We were both a bit groggy from the sudden jolt.

"What is that?!" I shouted over the blaring noise.

"The academy's emergency alarm!" he yelled back. He ran over to the door, still only in his underwear. He opened the door just enough so he could peek outside.

"Everyone is headed to the gym," he confirmed as he shut the door. "We gotta go."

We threw on our clothes as quickly as possible and sprinted out of his room. As we made our way to the gym, it became obvious that something was happening. Fannar and I held hands so we wouldn't get separated in the flood of people. The teachers were shouting orders for us to move "in a fast but orderly manner" as they shepherded us to the gym. Mostly, the students were fairly calm since we still weren't sure if this was a drill or a real emergency.

Before we knew it, we were in the gym, gathered among the two thousand other students. There was a nervous murmuring among the crowd, and I got on my tiptoes to peer around, searching for familiar faces.

"Iris and Guiden are over there!" I said to Fannar, and we made our way over to where they were standing.

"Do you know what's going on?" Fannar asked them.

"No, no one will tell us anything," Iris answered with a concerned look.

"Do you think it's a drill?" I asked.

"I don't think so," Guiden replied. "This seems much more serious."

"Last year when this happened, a basilisk got on campus," Fannar recalled.

"What's a basilisk?" I asked.

"A giant fire-breathing lizard," Iris answered.

My eyes widened. "Are you serious?!"

Guiden nodded toward the stage that had been set up at one end of the gym.

Oddly, I still hadn't seen Jimmy or Dawn when Headmaster Moira stepped in front of the microphone. She had a look on her face that made my blood run cold, and when she tapped the microphone, everyone fell silent. You could hear a pin drop as soon as she touched the mic.

"I am very sad to inform you all that several of our students were attacked by a horrendous beast last night just outside of the academy," Headmaster Moira said. "One student, Angela Conner, was almost killed."

The information created a palpable shockwave as a collective gasp rattled through the crowd.

That's the Angela from my training class.

My heart sank. Obviously, Angela had never been nice to me, but I certainly didn't wish harm upon her. Fannar's hand clenched near painfully over mine.

Headmaster Moira continued. "She would have succumbed to her wounds if she hadn't been brought quickly to the Healing Center by other students." She paused before continuing, "Unfortunately, the beast is still at large."

Another gasp rolled through the crowd, carrying a few squeaks and cries of terror.

"Please listen to me carefully," Headmaster Moira implored. "You must not leave campus until further notice. Our faculty is working to secure the academy's defenses. I assure you that the enchantments laid across the grounds are extremely effective. However, we cannot protect you once you leave campus. You must remain inside the academy's gates until we are sure the beast is no longer a threat."

Headmaster Moira retrieved a green gem, similar to the one I had seen before in her office, from her dress pocket. When she pressed it, it glowed, projecting a burst of light that formed into what I can only call a large hologram.

"This is what the beast looks like," Headmaster Moira said. "If you see it, you must tell a faculty member *immediately*."

The hulking figure in front of us was a horrifying sight—like a yeti, yet quadrupedal, with thick, shaggy white fur, large front legs with thick biceps, and comparatively scrawny back legs. Its face was almost like a human's, only missing a nose, with large shark-like teeth. Four eyes were glowing bright red, and its mouth hung open, frozen midway through a fearsome roar. I could practically hear its growl, feel the cold radiating from it. It gave me chills.

The crowd gave another gasp as they looked upon it—me amongst them—but Fannar stiffened next to me, as if he had turned to ice. I looked at him and saw a bit of cold fog swirling around his clenched, shaking fists. His frigid eyes were wide, and he looked like he was watching a train wreck happen right in front of him.

"Fannar?"

He didn't respond.

"Fannar!"

He jumped lightly and looked over at me.

"What is it?" I asked.

"That crest . . ."

I looked up at the beast again. I couldn't see any marks on it. "What crest?"

"The forehead."

I squinted to see the beast's forehead, where—barely visible—there was a little shield split into four sections. I couldn't quite discern what was in each of the sections, but Fannar looked at it with genuine recognition.

"So," I murmured, "does this mean . . . what I think it means?"

"Yes," Fannar replied. "My parents sent this thing . . . probably to kill you, Helena."

After the assembly, Fannar traversed the crowd and hurried toward the stage with me in tow.

"Headmaster Moira!" he called to her as she exited the stage.

"Fannar, if you are asking if I have more information—" Headmaster Moira began.

"No," Fannar interrupted. "I know why the beast is here."

"It's my fault!" I added urgently.

The headmaster thought a moment and said, "You two had better come with me." A black hole appeared in front of her, and she stepped through it. Fannar and I followed her.

The same horrible sensation passed over me as the first time I'd walked through one of the headmaster's portals, and both Fannar and I tumbled out into her office.

Headmaster Moira sat behind her desk again, like the day I arrived here, but she was clearly a lot less jovial than she was then.

"Talk," she barked before we had a chance to sit.

Fannar and I shared a glance. I swallowed but couldn't form any words.

"You know about us, right?" Fannar asked, motioning to me.

Headmaster Moira leaned back, her elbows resting on the arms of her chair, and pressed her fingertips together. "Yes, of course. I don't meddle in the personal lives of our students if I can help it. You're both adults, after all—even if you do sometimes act like children. Is that what you think this monster attack is about?"

"My parents sent it to hurt Helena," Fannar said angrily. "I'm sure of it."

"This makes more sense now," Headmaster Moira explained. "From what we can tell, it's specifically targeting Fire Enchanted students."

"How can you be sure?" I asked, trying not to let my emotions show.

"The attack occurred in front of the movie theater," Headmaster Moira responded grimly. "A large group of students from all guilds gathered outside after the movie ended. According to witnesses, the beast only attacked Fire Enchanted students, ignoring everyone else."

"Oh my God," I gasped in horror, remembering that I hadn't seen Dawn and Jimmy at the assembly. "I think that's the movie Dawn and Jimmy wanted me to see with them." I frantically asked Headmaster Moira, fear and concern evident in my trembling voice, "Are they okay? Were they hurt?"

"Angela was the only one who had been seriously injured," she replied. "Everyone else is okay. Just some scrapes and bruises. They've already been treated and released from the Healing Center."

I let out a shaky breath as I thought about what could have happened to my friends . . . what could've happened to me. "I can't believe this. They were just having a fun night out."

My stomach dropped with a mix of anger and sadness at the senselessness of it all. It wasn't a coincidence that my guild was targeted specifically.

The headmaster continued, "I suspected that it came from the Ice Kingdom, but we couldn't be certain. I never thought that your parents would be so vindictive as to endanger the lives of all the Fire Enchanted students just to get revenge on one."

My heart hurt. I felt numb. It was starting to resonate with me: *this was **my** fault . . . People were hurt because of me. Someone **almost died** because of me.*

"I'm sorry," I whispered. "I'm so sorry."

I felt Fannar's presence as he stepped closer to me.

Headmaster Moira's face softened even more. "Don't apologize. You didn't do this."

Fannar put a hand on the small of my back. When I looked at him, he smiled sadly and nodded in agreement.

Then he looked up at the headmaster. "Headmaster Moira, you have to talk to my parents. I knew they wouldn't be happy about Helena, but I never thought they'd be willing to risk the lives of every Fire Enchanted at the academy! You need to convince them to stop this!"

"I can't do that, Fannar," she replied. Before we had a chance to protest, she continued. "You two decided to start a very politically problematic relationship, which you're well within your right to do, but for me to get involved in any way would go against the academy's neutral position. If I were to argue for a relationship between a Fire and Ice Enchanted on your behalf to the Ice Kingdom, this academy's neutrality would no longer be respected."

Fannar slumped into one of the headmaster's chairs in defeat.

"But isn't there something you can do?" I pleaded.

"I can do something about that beast without it being a political statement. After all, it is attacking my students. I don't need to know *why* it was sent here to deal with it. I'm confident that as soon as we find it, we will be able to destroy it. I already reached out to the Ice King and Queen when I first suspected it was from the Ice Kingdom, but of course, they denied any knowledge of it. Hopefully, that will send a message to your parents loud and clear to keep their disapproval of your taste in girlfriends off my campus. However . . ."

Fannar and I glanced at each other nervously.

She scanned a dark gaze over us both before continuing, "What I will say is that if the Ice Kingdom continues to attack the academy . . . well, then it makes you a safety hazard to the other students." Headmaster Moira leaned forward and linked her fingers as if she was about to give us bad news. "So you would both have to be expelled."

CHAPTER FIFTEEN

The idea of being threatened with expulsion when we had done nothing wrong almost sent me into a tizzy. I was about to burst into protest, but Fannar lightly touched my back to stop me.

"We understand," Fannar said. "Thank you, Headmaster Moira. Please let us know if there is anything we can do to help."

I turned and looked at him. He had his expressionless ice mask on again.

"Please don't speak of this to anyone," the headmaster requested. "Only the faculty knows the beast is targeting Fire Enchanted, and we don't want to cause a panic among the Fire Guild, nor do we want the other students to let down their guard. It's best if all students remain on campus until the beast is caught." She nodded to dismiss us. "Be safe!"

We walked out of her office and back toward the dorms. As soon as we left the administration building, I turned to Fannar.

"What was that about?" I asked.

Fannar shrugged. "There's no use in arguing with her. We just have to make sure you stay on campus where it's safe until they catch the beast and hope the headmaster can put enough pressure on my parents to not do it again."

I really didn't like the sound of that. I never depended on other people to solve my problems. I couldn't imagine that the best course of action would be to hide from the beast and do nothing while other Fire Enchanted could get hurt or killed because it wanted *me*.

What if the beast managed to get through the academy's defenses? What if an errant or ignorant student went off-campus?

A surge of determination filled me, and I balled my hand into a tight fist as my passion and actual fire radiated from me.

"I'll go," I finally said.

His eyes widened. "What do you mean 'go'?"

"Leave the academy. It's ultimately looking for me, right? So it'll follow me and won't come back here."

Fannar stepped in front of me, eyes burning. "You are not leaving. It will kill you once you set foot off campus!"

"I'm not going to hide here until it finally kills someone else! If I'm going to be expelled anyway, I'd rather leave on my terms so no one else gets hurt!"

Fannar spent a second reading my expression. He sighed a little and shook his head.

"Fine," he said, "Stubborn Fire Enchanted, we'll go."

"We?" I asked.

He took my hand. "Of course, *we.*" He looked down, scowling in anger and pain. "Everything my sister and I have ever done was to make our parents proud and be the perfect royals we're supposed to be. Look where it got her." Then, he looked at me again. "But now I have you. You are the only thing in my life that makes me truly happy. I'm not giving up on us. I don't care how much my parents hate it. I'm going to fight for us."

"We are going to fight for us together. If your parents want to break us up, they'll need to do better than a furry snow monster!" I declared with a smirk. "And after we get through this, we'll go help Gwyneira! We'll fight every damn kingdom if we have to! I'm not scared!"

He shook his head, laughing at me. "You're incredible." He gazed at me with those deep blue eyes. "I love you, Helena."

"I love you, too. We're going to get through this together."

We shared a smooch as we reached the girls' dorm and saw Guiden and Iris outside.

"There you are!" Iris said. "I saw you guys leave with Headmaster Moira. What happened?"

"The beast was sent here by my parents to kill Helena," Fannar said.

"What?!" Guiden and Iris both yelled.

I nodded sadly. "We're going to leave the academy."

"You can't do that!" Iris exclaimed. "It's after you! This is the only safe place."

"If I leave, I can draw it away from here," I explained. "I don't want anyone else to get hurt. I can't have that on my conscience."

"I know you said that your parents wouldn't be happy about you two being together, but this is crazy," Guiden said, astonished.

"If anything, we gave them a good reason to kill as many Fire Enchanted as possible." Fannar shook his head in hatred.

"But don't they care that Helena is—" Iris began but looked at me as if asking permission to continue.

To be honest, I was not a hundred percent sure what she was about to say. No one else seemed to have a clue either, because both Fannar's and Guiden's gazes moved between her and me.

"Because she's what?" Fannar asked her.

"Because she's got a Combined Enchanted mark!" Iris exploded. "She's a Combined Fire and Ice Enchanted! After Helena showed me her mark, I did some research in the library. They're basically nonexistent nowadays. Maybe your parents will be accepting of her because she's clearly a rare breed of Fire Enchanted."

Fannar scoffed, "It never helped *me* with my parents."

"What?!" Iris gasped. Guiden's eyebrow arched with curiosity.

Fannar pulled down his shirt collar, then ran his hand under his collarbone, revealing his snowflake mark with the volcano inside of it.

"You have a combined mark, too?!" Iris gasped. "Maybe I was wrong about how rare they are?"

"No," Fannar said, releasing his collar. "I'd never heard of another one until I met Helena."

"Either way, I don't see how leaving the academy is a good idea," Guiden said. "Where would you even go?"

Fannar looked at me and said, "I don't think we thought that far ahead yet."

"What about the Fire Kingdom?" I asked. "That's where I'm supposed to be from, right?"

Fannar chuckled. "Yes, but it's probably not a good idea for *me* to go there."

"The Unenchanted Realm?" I offered.

"Bad idea," Guiden said. "What if the beast follows you there?"

"I just need to get away from here as soon as possible," I said.

Iris piped up. "Why don't you go to the Earth Kingdom? As far as I know, we don't have any major problems with the Fire or Ice Kingdoms at the moment. You'll be able to hide out there."

"Yes!" Guiden agreed, his eyes lighting up. "I live in a pretty remote part of the kingdom, far away from the capital, so it should be pretty quiet. My parents love all of my friends, even the non-Earth ones."

Fannar and I looked at each other with hope. I nodded.

Fannar nodded determinedly. "You know," he said firmly, "I think we'll take you up on that offer, at least until the beast is caught and we know my parents aren't a threat to Helena."

Guiden nodded. "You can stay as long as you need to."

"How do we get to the Earth Kingdom?" I asked.

Iris's lips twisted into a half-frown. "Without one of the headmaster's portals, you'll have to use the shared portals in Henristead. It's on the other side of the forest outside of the academy. It's still going to be dangerous, especially with the beast out there."

Fannar nodded in agreement. "But at least we have a plan."

"We really need to go now," I urged. "The longer I stay here, the more I put others at risk."

"Okay," Iris said and hugged me. "Please be careful! Have Guiden's mother send us word when you get there."

"We will. Thank you for everything." I looked at Iris and Guiden. "Both of you."

Guiden draped one of his arms over Iris's shoulders. "I'll tell my mom that you're coming and let her know if anything changes here. Take care, you two."

Fannar and I waved to our friends and began down the pathway to the edge of the academy.

By now, as Headmaster Moira had explained, the main gate was heavily guarded to keep the beast off-campus. We found a middle section of the academy perimeter that wasn't guarded, only protected by an enchantment keeping the beast out. Fannar summoned a mountain of ice that would allow us to climb over the wall.

"Are you sure you want to do this?" he asked with concern. "This beast, hiding from my parents in the Earth Kingdom . . . We're in for a heavy fight, Helena."

"And we'll give them as heavy a fight as they fucking want," I said with determination, looking him straight in the eyes. "We'll win or die trying, as long as we do it together."

He held his hand out to me. "Ready?" he asked.

We intertwined our fingers, and we walked over the academy wall hand in hand.

It occurred to me right then that I had never been outside the academy. Not really. I walked around campus, the courtyards, and the training fields, but we were always surrounded by large castle-like walls. Haven Academy was a safe bubble, and here we were, intentionally leaving that security behind.

The thick forest canopy covered the sky like a dark green blanket, with only faint rays of sunlight peeking through. The trees' broad trunks stood tall and proud, blocking out any view of the world beyond, seemingly going on for miles. The scent of musty earth and decaying leaves hung in the air. Moss and ferns were scattered across the ground, and shadows played across the foliage as the wind passed through.

We carefully listened as we traversed through the woods, making our way to Henristead, alert to the presence of anything that could be dangerous in our vicinity. The eerie silence was oppressive, making it feel even more isolated. The crunch of our footsteps echoed in the stillness. There were no other sounds except for the occasional birds chirping or the wind whistling around us.

Roughly an hour had passed when suddenly, a loud, thunderous roar broke the silence in the forest above us.

"Helena, look out!" Fannar yelled.

An avalanche of snow slammed into my side, knocking me through the air, and I slid to the ground a few feet away from where I had been walking. Fannar had pushed me out of the way with his powers. I shoved my feet under me and heaved myself up.

We found ourselves standing face-to-face with the four-eyed yeti from the headmaster's hologram projection. It slowly padded around to face me, all four of its blood-red eyes focusing on me. I froze in fear. Fannar soared up into the sky, a ramp of ice under his feet. He summoned a frozen javelin and threw it at the yeti. It crashed into the back of the creature's head.

"NO! You look at ME!" he screamed.

As the monster looked away from me, I sprinted away from its line of sight. I heard Fannar launch a few more attacks—then there was a crack. He screamed.

"Fannar!"

His name slipped out of my mouth before I could stop it.

A pulse of panic rushed through me. I forced two big fireballs into my hands, then flung them both at the beast.

As they hit the monster, it dropped from its front paws onto the forest floor, screeching in agony. Then it turned its crimson gaze back on me.

"Helena!"

Then, an icy arm clasped around my waist and dragged me up. When I got my bearings, I realized Fannar and I were flying atop a ramp of ice he was summoning.

We soared over the head of the beast, and it swatted at us like a cat. But it didn't reach us.

"Helena!" Fannar snapped. "Throw some fire down there!"

I slapped my hands and rubbed them together. They burst into flames. "Coming right up!"

I thrust my palms forward, and jets of fire exploded out from my hands and onto the creature. The yeti howled as the molten power poured down onto its head. Fannar carried us around the beast's head in a circle.

It screamed, thrashing around in the blaze.

"It's working!" Fannar called.

Then the beast made a swipe—but not at us. It clawed at one of the pillars holding the ramp.

The ice shuddered beneath us. Fannar staggered.

Another strike to the pillars holding us. There was a worrying dip. Fannar gripped me harder.

One more strike—and we dropped.

We tumbled. I screamed. Fannar pulled me into his chest, cold radiating from him.

I turned into his chest, the sickening weightlessness overtaking me. I howled as we tumbled through the air.

We then crunched into a pile of snow, unharmed.

Oh . . . oh, thank God!

"Helena!"

As I opened my eyes, a giant paw hovered over my head. Everything was happening so fast that I didn't have time to react. Fannar grabbed me and tried to roll both of us away from the beast, but he wasn't fast enough. Sharp claws raked across my back.

"AH!"

"Helena!"

A crash shuddered through the ground, and I looked up to see a bubble of ice caging me. The beast beat on the ice dome over me, and through the mottled frozen water, I watched Fannar zip around, throwing more icy spears at the monster.

It got distracted and lumbered after Fannar, growling.

I sprinted to the wall of my ice cage—then realized there was no way out for me.

"Let me out!"

Damn it, Fannar!

I slammed my hands on the side of the ice, but he ignored me. Just as the beast couldn't get in, I couldn't get out.

Wait . . . the monster wouldn't be able to get out either if it was in here!

The plan in my head formed quickly. I clenched my fists, and more heat burned in my palms. I pressed my hands against the ice prison and melted the walls thin enough for me to run my shoulder into it and break out.

"*Fannar!*" I screamed, "I have an idea!"

He was only a short distance away, but I wasn't sure if he could hear me—he swooped around, skating through the air, throwing ice attacks.

The beast shook the ice off easily, with only the sharpest of Fannar's spears piercing the beast's shoulders.

I sprinted toward the fray. I summoned another fireball and flung it at the creature. It flinched and yelped as it was hit, and Fannar finally noticed me. The creature lumbered toward me, but Fannar swooped down faster than it could get to me. I was prepared this time when he seized me around the waist and dragged me up into the air.

As we flew around, Fannar explained, "I can't move faster than it can with both of us! We're going to have to keep jumping!"

"Right!"

"Ready? *Jump!*"

We both jumped. The ramp vanished for a moment—just as the beast slashed at the ramp we were just on.

We fell for a moment and then hit a second ramp and kept going as the dumb beast kept attacking where we had just been.

"Fannar, I have a plan!" I said quickly.

"What is it?"

"It couldn't break through the barrier you put around me! You can trap it!"

"It will break through eventually if it has enough time," Fannar answered, but then he brightened. "But it can't break through if it's frozen solid! That's it! Remember how I said I was going to freeze Fire douche's legs and shatter them? It would take me too long to freeze the beast's whole body by myself, but if you melt my ice, we can completely soak it in water first, and I can freeze it a lot faster."

I took an excited breath as I began to understand what Fannar was suggesting. "And once it's frozen solid, I'll break it!"

"Exactly!" Fannar said back with a smirk.

The creature turned its attention back to us. It lumbered over with a roar and raised a large paw.

"*Jump!*" Fannar barked.

We both jumped just as the paw cracked the ramp we were on. Fannar caught us on a second ramp. "You ready?" he asked.

I clapped my hands and rubbed them. Exhaustion was starting to set in, and it was taking more and more effort to light my hands on fire.

"Ready when you were!" I replied.

"Alright . . . *go!*"

I summoned the largest fireball that I could and shot it toward the monster. Fannar did the same with a blustering cloud of ice particles.

Our powers combined into a torrent of water on the creature. After only seconds, it was already starting to frost the tips of its fur.

"Fannar, it was already freezing!"

"Keep going!" he ordered. "This is going to work!"

We continued our magical onslaught, and the creature became completely soaked from head to tail.

"Now stop!" Fannar barked.

I did—I was glad to rest for a moment. My heart was hammering, and I was dripping in sweat.

Then, with a deep grunt, Fannar's freezing cloud intensified, and the water drenching its body turned into clear ice. The yeti stopped for a moment, then the ice around its joints cracked. It kept moving.

But it was moving slower than it was before.

"One more time! Let's go!"

I had to summon more strength. For him.

Again, he summoned a gust of white ice shards, and it fell onto the beast. It began freezing on top of the ice that we had already laid. The monster slowed even more, weighed down.

"Now!" I ordered. "Freeze it again!"

Fannar blasted it with another freezing ray. Again, the ice around its joints began to break, but it only cracked this time, and the monster was struggling to move.

"One more time!" I insisted.

Fannar nodded.

Once more, we both poured out our powers, another dose of water on the beast—and Fannar froze it. This blast lasted longer than ever, as more and more ice built up over its entire body. The beast froze solid, becoming a statue of ice.

Finally, Fannar stopped, gasping for air.

My hands clasped together in an L-shape, forming my "fire gun", and took a deep breath. Exhaustion weighed heavily on me, making it difficult to find any more strength within myself. A guttural cry escaped my throat as I tapped into the last reserves of energy within me, channeling them through my fingers.

A blinding shot of white rocketed out and into the heart of the beast. It cracked through in a perfect shot, and those cracks spread throughout the ice statue. Then, it fell apart into bloody shards of ice.

It was done.

A quiet disbelief hung in the air for what seemed like an eternity, as if we weren't sure if we could celebrate yet. I turned to say something to Fannar when his arms unexpectedly wrapped around me in a tight hug.

"We did it!" he proclaimed, his eyes alight in excitement.

I laughed. Fannar's rare exuberance was infectious.

He pulled me in closer, and his cool lips touched mine.

"We did it," I repeated, smiling.

Fannar's expression suddenly changed to worry as he pulled away from me. He looked at his hands, which had red smears of blood on them, and then looked at my back.

"Helena," he said with concern. "You're still bleeding
. . ."

"I am?" The adrenaline was beginning to wear off, and long streaks of pain ran down my back where the beast had scratched me.

"We should go back to the academy," Fannar suggested. "We need to get you healed. We can let Headmaster Moira know that we killed the beast and that everyone is safe . . . at least for now."

"So maybe we won't be expelled?" I considered. The pain flared sharply, and I winced. "My back is killing me."

"Let me see," Fannar pulled my shirt up over my back and examined my wounds. "Hold still." He held his hands over the wounds and began to cool my back until it was fairly numb. "Does that feel better?"

"It does. Thanks."

"It's only temporary. You need a healer."

I nodded.

Fannar scooped me up into his arms.

"You don't have to do that! I can walk just fine!" I giggled.

"I know," he smirked at me and skated us back toward the academy.

CHAPTER SIXTEEN

"I can't believe it!" Iris gasped in joy. "Headmaster Moira said that faculty members killed the beast."

We stood in a grassy area between the administration building and the library. A light breeze blew through the trees, rustling their leaves softly. Headmaster Moira had already announced that the beast had been killed and that the lockdown order was lifted. The surrounding students were back to their normal lives, mingling with each other or hurrying to their next classes.

"No, it was us!" I insisted.

"Of course, she didn't tell anyone that we did it," Fannar stated. "Students weren't supposed to leave campus, and if anyone found out that we killed it, she might have to explain why it came here."

"Do you know what your parents are going to do now?" Guiden asked.

Fannar shook his head. "Not yet."

"We don't even know if we're still going to be expelled," I said, giving Fannar a worried look.

"Headmaster Moira is supposed to talk to my parents, and she said she'll let us know once she's made a decision," Fannar said.

Iris frowned. "You don't think they would really try to kill Helena again, do you?"

"Not if the headmaster has anything to say about it," Guiden said. "She's a pretty scary lady herself."

"Well, if we get expelled, at least we have a place to go." I looked at Guiden gratefully.

"Anytime," he nodded and then smirked. "Who would have thought fire and ice, huh? You two have really messed with the order of things."

"I love it!" Iris cheered. "So romantic! Whatever you two need, we'll be here!"

Fannar and I smiled at each other, and I turned back to Iris and Guiden.

"Thanks, guys," I said gratefully.

I glanced again at Fannar. He was silent, but his expression spoke volumes. He was overwhelmed by the wave of support from our friends. His grateful smile said it all.

At that moment, a small black flash of light appeared in front of us. It spread out into a hologram of Headmaster Moira's face.

"Helena and Fannar," the hologram said. "I'm ready for you."

"Yes, Headmaster," Fannar said. "We'll be right there."

The hologram disappeared.

I looked at Fannar, and he cast me a nervous look in return.

"Here we go," I murmured.

"Good luck," Guiden said.

Iris squeezed me and crossed her fingers. "It's going to be fine," she tried to reassure me. "See you soon."

Once Fannar and I made it to Headmaster Moira's office door, we found her sitting behind her desk, hands linked and a somewhat tense smile on her face.

"Ah, you two. Come in!"

We both walked inside, and, with a wave of her hand, the headmaster closed the door behind us. We sat down in the chairs in front of her desk.

"First of all, I want to commend you on your bravery and effectiveness in dealing with the beast," she began. "While I suggest that you don't do anything that dangerous ever again, the academy appreciates your ambition to keep other students safe."

We nodded.

"I do have some good news," she continued. "I spoke with Fannar's parents. While they admitted to no wrongdoing, they agreed not to release any beasts or make any attempts on Helena's life. Of course, I still believe they are responsible for the appearance of the beast, despite their denials."

Fannar didn't look like he was so sure.

"Really?" I asked with a spark of hope.

"Yes," the headmaster confirmed. "That means the two of you no longer pose a threat to other students and will not be expelled. In fact, you will be welcome next semester with open arms."

I grinned. Fannar let out a sigh of relief, then smiled at me.

"Thank you, Headmaster Moira!" I chirped.

"Yes, thank you very much," Fannar said.

The headmaster smiled warmly at us but continued, "However, the Ice King and Queen have requested that you and Fannar return to the Ice Kingdom for winter break."

What?!

Fannar's eyes widened in fear. "*Both* of us? As in . . . Helena, too?"

Headmaster Moira nodded. "Yes."

"No!" Fannar exploded. "They're going to kill her! We can't bring Helena to my parents!"

Headmaster Moira held up her hand to silence him and said, "Let me explain. Iris let me know something about you two, which swayed the negotiations somewhat." She linked her hands together and peered over her knuckles at the pair of us. "You two have the marks of Combined Enchanted, possibly the rarest Enchanted that exist in this world."

"My parents know that about me," Fannar said, confused. "Why would they care about Helena also being a Combined Enchanted?"

"Now they understand what a Combined Enchanted is," Headmaster Moira answered. "It appears they had no idea that an Enchanted could have the strength to control the powers of two Guilds at once. And now, you've found another to bring home. If they let you continue your relationship, they'll have two of them in their kingdom."

"I get it," Fannar said bitterly. "Now that they know Helena's extremely powerful and a rare Combined Enchanted, they've realized how *useful* she can be."

Headmaster Moira shrugged. "I cannot say for certain, but knowing your parents, yes. I'm sure they see her as a political boon, if not a military asset, to the Ice Kingdom."

Fannar gave a bitter grunt.

"But it was what I had to tell them to save her life. If I didn't, she wouldn't have survived three steps outside the academy without another assassination attempt, as they would feel even more threatened if Helena went to the Fire Kingdom." The headmaster pursed her lips together. "So, that leaves you both with a choice as to whether you'll return to the Ice Kingdom, as they've requested. I can't make that decision for you, but, for your own safety, it seems like the best thing to do for now."

Fannar looked at me. There were a hundred things in his polar eyes, but he said nothing.

"Well, I imagine you both need some time to think about it. Regardless, you are both welcome back next year."

"Thank you, Headmaster Moira," I said. "We appreciate your help."

"Good luck," she said.

After that, we were dismissed and left the headmaster's office, making our way back to the dorms. Fannar walked stone-faced and silent, so I pulled him off the pathway and onto a bench under a tree.

"You haven't said a word," I spoke nervously, leaning in and holding one of his hands. "We need to talk about this."

Fannar looked down, his eyebrows knitting together lightly. "It's going to be dangerous. I have to go back to the Ice Kingdom, but . . ." He gazed at me with worry in his frosty eyes. "I don't know what my parents have in store for you, Helena. You could still go to the Earth Kingdom with Guiden and Iris."

"I'm not letting you go back and deal with this alone," I responded. "You heard what Headmaster Moira said. They want both of us. If I don't go, we risk them going after other Fire Enchanted again, maybe even the entire Fire Kingdom."

Fannar sighed. "You're right."

"Of course I am," I smiled at him, trying to ease the tension, and wound my arms around him. "I'm a stubborn Fire Enchanted. Plus, we're the world's only Combined Enchanted! We need to stick together."

He chuckled as his hands wrapped around my waist and pulled me further into him. "We do, don't we?"

Fannar tucked a strand of hair behind my ear, his thumb lingering on my cheek, and lowered his face to mine. His ice-cold lips touched mine, and I was drawn back into the same ecstatic feeling as when we first kissed. He wrapped me in his arms and held me close, not letting anything come between us. I felt brighter than all the flames that I had ever created. At that moment, I felt complete.

Winter break was still three weeks away. The Ice Kingdom would have to wait until we finished our final exams first. We didn't know what the future held for us, but we were determined to weather any storm that came our way.

As we walked back to the dorms, we stepped boldly into our fate, side by side, forever linked by our unwavering bond.

EPILOGUE

Stepping through the grand entrance of the Ice Castle, I marveled at the sheer beauty surrounding us. The castle rose tall and majestic, its walls gleaming with shimmering blue and white ice. Crystalline spires adorned its towers, sparkling brilliantly in the sun. Intricately carved windows refracted the light into a dazzling display, as snow-covered turrets and balconies added to the fairytale-like atmosphere. A pristine blanket of glistening snow enveloped the entire castle grounds, creating a magical, frozen wonderland.

However, my awe quickly faded as the bitter cold seeped into my bones. As requested by Fannar's parents, we traveled to the Ice Kingdom to spend our winter break. Despite wearing the warmest clothes I owned, I shivered uncontrollably and stumbled on the slippery floor more than once. Each time I heard a pop or groan from the glacial walls, I jumped in unease.

One of the servants handed Fannar a thick fur blanket. "For the lady," he said with a slight bow.

"Here," Fannar said softly, draping the heavy white fur over my shoulders.

"Thanks," I murmured, my warm breath clouding in front of me as it mingled with the frigid air. I wrapped the fur around my body as tightly as I could.

Fannar grasped my hand in his, guiding me through the grand hall of the castle. The walls, crafted from glistening transparent ice, displayed intricate carvings of mythical creatures and ethereal unicorns. Above us, an expansive ceiling boasted a breathtaking display of arched windows and shimmering chandeliers, casting a dazzling array of colors and patterns throughout the vast chamber.

"Your Royal Highness. My lady." The staff lowered their gaze and bowed as we passed by.

It was odd to see Fannar addressed as "Your Royal Highness". Since everyone at the academy treated him no differently than any other student, I frequently forgot that he was actually a prince.

"Almost there," he said softly. "After we talk to my parents, we can just relax in my room until dinner."

I steeled myself as we approached an ornate set of doors. Beyond them waited the king and queen—Fannar's parents.

My heart pounded, palms sweating despite the chill. I had no idea what to expect from them, other than hostility. After all, they were the ones who unleashed the monster to eliminate me. Would they have me thrown in the dungeon? Would they attack me on sight?

Sensing my trepidation, Fannar gave my hand a reassuring squeeze. "Don't worry, I'm right here. I won't let them do anything to you." His eyes locked onto mine, filled with unwavering determination, his voice steady, calming my nerves slightly. "Remember the plan. If they try anything, we leave right away and go back to the academy."

"Right." I nodded.

Still, I tensed as the doors swung open. The translucent walls of the opulent throne room reflected the light from sparkling chandeliers, creating a dazzling glow that bathed the entire chamber. Elaborate ice sculptures sat in every corner, their frozen beauty capturing the essence of the Ice Kingdom. Intricate carvings of glaciers and snowflakes adorned the sweeping arches and pillars of glittering ice.

My initial awe was quickly replaced by apprehension as I caught sight of Fannar's parents. The Ice King sat on his throne, his silver hair perfectly coiffed and piercing blue eyes locked onto us. Beside him, the Ice Queen appeared as though she had been carved from ice herself—her long white hair styled elegantly, crowned with icicles that shimmered like diamonds.

"Your Majesties, Lady Helena of the Unenchanted Realm," the royal herald announced.

I started to curtsy as Fannar showed me earlier, but to my surprise, the Ice Queen rose from her throne and approached us with a warm smile that contradicted everything I'd been told about her.

She clasped my hands in hers, her cool touch surprisingly gentle. "Helena, my dear, you are even more beautiful than we've heard. Look at that beautiful red hair and those green eyes! Simply stunning!"

"Uh, thank you, Your Majesty," I stammered, taken aback by her unexpected friendliness.

"Chairs, please." The Ice King gestured his hand in the air.

Two staff members stepped forward and pointed their hands to an empty space in front of Fannar and me. They instantly formed two chairs of solid ice.

Now, that's handy. Too bad a fire chair wouldn't be as practical.

"Please, have a seat," the Ice King said.

The Ice Queen noticed my shivering, despite Fannar's earlier efforts. "Bring spiced cider and more furs," the Ice

Queen requested of the servants. "Lady Helena is our guest. Make sure she is comfortable."

"Yes, Your Majesty."

As we settled into our seats, servants brought steaming cups of fragrant mulled cider and placed two more layers of furs on my shoulders. I wrapped my hands around the cup, grateful for the additional warmth it provided.

"So, you are a Fire Enchanted but not from the Fire Kingdom?" Fannar's father asked with slight skepticism.

"Yes, Your Majesty," I replied. "I grew up in the Unenchanted Realm and never been to the Fire Kingdom. Your kingdom is the first one I've visited in the Enchanted Realm."

"What is the Unenchanted Realm like?" the Ice Queen asked, her eyes sparkling with genuine interest.

"Actually, it's a lot like Haven Academy . . . but without magic, powers, or gremlins." I laughed.

"That sounds nothing like the Enchanted Realm!"

I shrugged and chuckled. "Okay, I guess not."

The Ice King laughed loudly. Fannar, however, furrowed his brow and narrowed his eyes, showing his suspicion with their surprisingly warm reception.

Fannar's mother leaned in, peppering me with more questions about the Unenchanted Realm and my studies at the academy.

"The headmaster informed us of how quickly you rose to the top of your class, even though it has only been a few months since your powers manifested," the Ice King said. "You must be very proud of everything you achieved."

I smiled. "Thank you. Fannar gets a lot of credit for his help in training with me."

"Another cup of cider for the lady!" The Ice King motioned for a servant to refill my cup. "We want to ensure our guest is well taken care of."

As I took another slow sip of my spiced cider, I glanced at Fannar, who still scrutinized his parents' every word from the corner of his eye. His grip on his cup tightened, betraying his inner turmoil. I knew he sensed that something was off, but for now, I was just grateful for their unlikely hospitality and the fact that I could peacefully sip on hot cider without having to fight for my life.

Fannar cleared his throat loud enough to draw the attention of everyone in the throne room. His eyes narrowed and his lips pressed tightly together as he finally addressed his parents.

"Speaking of the academy," Fannar started sharply, "did you send that quad-eyed yeti to the academy to attack Fire Enchanted?"

The Ice King and Queen exchanged glances, their smiles faltering for just a moment before they regained their composure.

"Of course not, son," the king replied.

"Goodness, no. Why would we do such a thing?" the queen asked. "We certainly had no part in any attack."

Fannar's eyes flashed. "Yet, the creature bore our royal crest. How do you explain that?"

The king waved his hand dismissively. "Clearly the work of some rebel faction."

"And it just happened to target Fire Enchanted after the news got out that I started dating Helena?"

"Purely a coincidence," Fannar's mother suggested sweetly.

"Coincidence?" Fannar scoffed, clearly unconvinced. "Seems rather unlikely, don't you think?"

The Ice King cleared his throat. "Regardless," he intervened, his tone firm and commanding, "we are simply relieved to hear that both of you managed to defeat such a fearsome creature."

I blinked in surprise. Headmaster Moira had told everyone the faculty killed the yeti, and we never told Fannar's parents that we were the ones that defeated it.

Fannar's fists clenched. "How very convenient you know nothing about it," he said coldly.

"Indeed," the Ice Queen chimed in, her ice-blue eyes wide with feigned innocence. "When we heard about the attacks, we were horrified." Her gaze fixed on me with awe. "Helena, you must be so powerful to have taken down such a monstrous beast. Your abilities are truly impressive."

"Uh, thank you," I murmured, my stomach churning with unease. "But it was a joint effort with Fannar."

"Of course." The Ice King nodded solemnly. "I imagine that the two of you make a formidable team." His tone made it clear the subject was closed.

The tension between Fannar and his parents grew thicker, and I found myself holding my breath, waiting for him to explode.

"What about Gwyneira?" Fannar snapped, his jaw set and his eyes blazing with anger.

The Ice King and Queen's welcoming smiles morphed into stern, icy glares.

"You sent her away to marry the Storm Prince, even though I warned you about him," Fannar continued. "He has a reputation for being cruel and ruthless!"

"Son, that was a decision made for the good of our kingdom," the Ice King replied calmly, his cold gaze locked onto Fannar's. "It was a necessary alliance."

"Have you heard anything from her?" Fannar pressed, his voice rising in pitch. "Do you even know if she's alive?"

The queen waved her hand airily. "We have been preoccupied with matters pertaining to our own kingdom and have not been in contact with your sister or the Storm Prince," she admitted, her voice devoid of emotion.

Fannar clenched his fists so tightly that the veins bulged in his thick forearms. His nostrils flared as he struggled to control his emotions. "You're not worried at all? She's your daughter!"

"Your sister is no longer our concern, Fannar," the Ice King said dismissively, his voice as cold as the ice that encased his throne. "She is fulfilling her duty as a princess of our kingdom."

My stomach twisted in knots. Fannar's parents' indifference towards Gwyneira's fate seemed almost cruel. My heart ached for Fannar, knowing the depth of love his love for his sister.

"Is that really how little she means to you?" Fannar growled, his eyes narrowing into slits. "Just another pawn to be used for political gain?"

"Enough!" The Ice Queen's voice sliced through the argument like a blade. "We have done what we must for the good of our people. You will become the future king and should understand that better than anyone!"

A heavy silence fell in the room, punctuated only by the crackling of the icy walls and the distant howl of the wind outside. The air felt colder than ever, and I shivered involuntarily, my breath visible in front of me.

"Be that as it may," the Ice King said at last, his eyes never leaving Fannar's, "the matter is settled. We will not discuss it further."

Hurt and betrayal flashed across Fannar's face. He struggled to keep his emotions in check, his body rigid with tension.

"Babe," I whispered, reaching out to grasp his arm.

He trembled with rage under my touch. I met his eyes pleadingly.

"Father. Mother," Fannar sneered, his tone dripping with disdain as he dipped his head per protocol.

Then, he spun around on his heel and stormed out of the throne room, as the king and queen's steely gaze followed his every step.

"Your Majesties." I curtsied respectfully before hurrying after Fannar, his footsteps echoing off the frozen walls.

The furs on my shoulders weighed down on me as I twisted through the icy corridors.

"Fannar, wait!" I called after him.

But he didn't slow down or look back, his anger propelling him forward like a force of nature. Plus, he knew that I could keep up. I finally caught up to him on a balcony overlooking a frozen fjord. Fannar gripped the railing, knuckles white. His shoulders heaved with each breath.

"Babe?" I approached cautiously. "Are you okay?"

Fannar laughed bitterly. "My parents just admitted they have no idea if my sister is alive and, frankly, they don't seem to care. So no, I'm pretty damn far from okay."

I leaned on the railing next to him, unsure of what to say. Below us, sunlight glinted off jagged icebergs bobbing silently in the water.

"At least they didn't try to kill me again, right?" I tried to lighten the mood.

He chuckled. "Yeah, I guess that's true. I've never seen them so friendly, not even to royal diplomats. That was really weird." He turned to look at me, his eyes filled with angry determination. "I just can't believe how heartless they can be towards their own daughter. That monster could be hurting Gwyneira. I can't just sit back and do nothing while my parents play their political games."

"I get it." I reached out and placed a comforting hand on his back, feeling the tension in his muscles slowly ease. "We'll find her, Fannar. We'll get her back."

"We can't. It could start a war with the Storm Kingdom."

"Then we'll figure something out. At least how to contact her. I promise."

Fannar's eyes glistened with hope. "You think so?"

I took his hand, lacing our fingers together. "I know so. We'll make sure your sister's okay."

Fannar let out a shaky breath and pulled me into a fierce embrace. We stayed locked together under the frigid sky, drawing strength from one another. Tomorrow we would make plans to find Gwyneira. But for now, all we could do was hope.

No matter what dangers awaited us, we could get through it as long as Fannar and I were together.

~～⌒

The story continues in *Taken by the Storm Prince*!

The strings of fate get tangled when Fannar's sister, Gwyneira, is forced into an arranged marriage with the grumpy, gorgeous Storm Prince.

Turn the page for a special preview.

SPECIAL PREVIEW - TAKEN BY THE STORM PRINCE

Haven Academy: Book 2

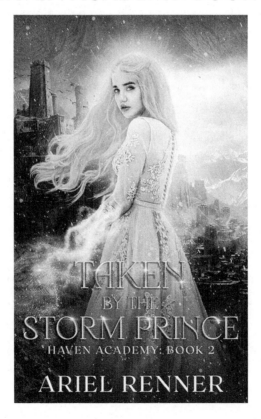

The chandelier above cast a warm glow as I ran my duster across the ornate wooden bookshelf, sending particles of dust dancing in the air. The opulent palace library had become one of my favorite places to clean since arriving at the Storm Castle two weeks prior. Ancient tomes and scrolls filled its floor-to-ceiling shelves. From the far corner of the library where I stood, I had an excellent view of a cloudy mid-afternoon sky through the tall windows. The scent of old parchment, wood polish, and leather filled my nostrils as I continued my task.

I remembered how grateful I would be when Fannar used to sneak one or two books into my room, allowing me to escape the confines of my tower and explore the world beyond its walls. I never dreamed of seeing thousands upon thousands of books like this. *Be careful not to damage any of these precious books, Gwyn.* I thought to myself, recalling the stern warning from the castle's head housekeeper. These were the treasures of the Storm Kingdom, after all.

As I carefully brushed the duster along a row of book spines, the heavy oak doors creaked open, and my eyes darted toward the entrance. Prince Brontes strode into the room with intent. His stormy gray eyes intensely scanned the vast collection of books like they were searching for prey.

My heart skipped a beat. I'd barely seen him since my first day in the castle, and I hadn't spoken to him since then either. I quickly averted my gaze and attempted to focus on my duties, hoping he wouldn't notice me all the way in the back of the library.

Brontes huffed under his breath with frustration. He paced around the room, the pounding of his boots echoing against the marble floor. One moment, he appeared calm and collected. The next, his brows furrowed, and he cursed quietly, as if attempting to contain a tempest within him.

My mind began to wander as I watched him from the corner of my eye. Despite my better judgment, I found myself fascinated by him. He had a noble aura about him, and yet there was something almost wild in his energy, like an animal pacing in its cage.

His strong arms reached for a book on a high shelf, and an unfamiliar warmth stirred within me. His unruly mane of dark hair cascaded over his forehead, making me want to run my fingers through it. The impossibly broad expanse of his shoulders stretched taut against the fabric of his shirt. For a moment, I wanted nothing more than to feel the power of those strong arms under my fingertips, but I promptly reminded myself that he was a monster.

I quickly snapped myself out of it and shook my head to clear my thoughts. I couldn't imagine what the queen would do if I was caught daydreaming in the presence of the prince and *fantasizing about him,* no less! I scolded myself silently as I resumed dusting the shelves with more vigor than necessary.

"Ah, there it is!" he exclaimed a few minutes later, finally spotting his desired book.

His sudden outburst startled me, and my duster clattered to the floor. I winced. *So much for going unnoticed.*

Brontes turned sharply and demanded, "Who's there?"

I stepped forward so he could see me. "It's me, Your Highness," I said quietly, being sure to keep my eyes downcast and my voice as flat as possible, not to give away a hint of emotion. "I apologize if I disturbed you."

"No need to apologize, Princess," he said. "You weren't disturbing me. Have you been hiding here all along?"

"Not hiding." I bent down to retrieve the fallen duster. "Just dusting."

The thudding of his boots grew louder as he approached me. Inwardly, I braced myself, not knowing what to expect from him. When I straightened up, he was so close that I could feel the heat emanating from his body, and I froze in place.

"Well, you've done an excellent job dusting." His lips turned upward ever so slightly.

His gaze swept across the length of my body from the floor to my face, where it lingered for what felt like an eternity before finally meeting mine. His stormy blue eyes bore into me, probing deep into my soul.

My heart raced as I stared back at him, perplexed by his expression. Was his compliment genuine, or had he been mocking me, knowing full well that I was a princess being treated like a servant? Why did he look at me with such intensity? My head spun with questions muddled by uncertainty and confusion as I tried to understand what he meant.

As my cheeks burned from his gaze, I averted my eyes away from him, hoping that would calm the uncontrollable pounding of my heart in its cage. My mother's teachings echoed in my ears—*remain stoic, unemotional*. I schooled my expression into one of cool indifference.

"Is something wrong?" Brontes inquired, head tilting.

"Nothing's wrong," I replied, turning away to resume my dusting.

"Ah, yes," Brontes scoffed. "The perfect, emotionless princess. How could I forget? I shouldn't be surprised. Typical of your kind, I suppose. You are just as my parents described Ice Enchanted—stiff and detached."

A spark of anger ignited within me, but I refused to let it show. My duster continued its methodical path along the shelves, my face a mask of indifference.

Brontes prowled closer. "You think you're so superior, don't you?" he continued, his voice growing more aggressive. "Your icy powers have made you an empty, frozen shell."

I clenched my jaw, my hands gripping the feather duster tightly. My parents taught me well—emotions were a weakness, and I couldn't afford to show any. I would not give him the satisfaction of a reaction. Let the prince hurl himself against my walls. He would not find a way in.

"Tell me, Princess," Brontes sneered, as if he was trying to bait me into a reaction. "Do you ever tire of being so . . . cold? So utterly lifeless?"

His words cut through me like a knife as I battled to keep my face impassive. Though my heart screamed for me to defend myself, my upbringing silenced it. I let out a slow, controlled breath, trying to dispel the roiling emotions within me.

"Look at me when I'm speaking to you!" Brontes barked, stopping directly behind me.

My head snapped toward him with cold eyes, but my pulse quickened. His handsome features twisted into a cruel sneer. The thoughts of him being a violent monster stung my brain like a swarm of angry hornets. His own mother said he could hurt or kill me.

My heart raced in my chest as I stumbled back, unsure whether to run or stay and face his wrath. But despite all of this, something about him made me want to stay—something dangerous and alluring that pulsed beneath his skin like electricity. It pulled me toward him even as all logic screamed at me to flee.

Silence fell. His presence filled the room, as heavy and crackling as an oncoming storm. His gaze felt like a weight, pressing down in an effort to make me fold. I refused to look away or give any indication of weakness—no matter how much he tried to rattle me, I stood my ground and met his stare with quiet defiance.

"What use are you, anyway? A shadow in the background, devoid of any real substance. Perhaps you're more suited to serving as a mere decoration."

He circled me slowly, like a predator stalking its prey, and my pulse quickened in response.

"Are you just some robot my mother purchased to tidy up after the rest of the staff?" He bent forward ominously, eyes blazing like hot embers. "Or perhaps a plaything for my own entertainment?" His gargantuan frame cast a dark shadow over me, looming like a sinister mountain ready to crush me beneath its weight.

A plaything? How dare he speak to me this way!

My icy exterior struggled to hold back the torrent of emotions that threatened to spill over. The heat of his anger and challenge to my resolve only made my frigid façade harder to break. I was determined not to yield nor show him the vulnerability that he desired.

"Nothing?" he challenged, stepping closer to me. "Do you even care about anything at all?"

My mother's lessons echoed through my mind, *Remain calm, show no weakness, never let them see your true feelings.*

"Of course I do, Your Highness," I finally responded, still maintaining his piercing gaze. "I simply prefer to keep my emotions . . . contained."

"Contained?" Brontes laughed bitterly. "That's an understatement. I've seen glaciers with more warmth than you, *Princess*."

"Perhaps it's better that way. Emotions can be dangerous." As hard as I tried to remain calm, a tinge of annoyance seeped into my voice. "I do not see how my demeanor is any concern of yours, *Your Highness*."

"Isn't it?" he shot back, his eyes narrowing dangerously. "You're to be my wife, yet you act as if you're made of stone."

His words stung, but I couldn't let him know. As the raging fire of his frustration burned brighter, I refused to give into his determination to break me.

"Nothing else to say for yourself?" he taunted, his voice cold and cutting. "Fine. Just go back to your dusting. You're clearly incapable of any real conversation."

His dismissal felt like a slap in the face, but I swallowed the resentment and frustration, returning to my task. As I moved to dust another shelf, Brontes stomped over to the fireplace, his frustration evident in every step.

"You're devoid of any warmth or life. It's infuriating!" he bellowed furiously. "How does anyone expect me to marry a soulless statue?!"

My body stiffened at the sound of his roar echoing throughout the library, and I flinched as he kicked an innocent log into the fire. The fireplace hissed and popped as the flames conjured ominous shadows upon the walls. My face burned with anger, and suddenly, the floodgates finally broke.

I lifted my chin and locked eyes with him. "Better soulless than a monster."

The words were out before I could stop them. Brontes jerked back as though struck. All at once, the stormy rage in his eyes dimmed, and a mysterious expression flickered across his face that looked like the dark cloud that hung over us.

In the silence that followed my accusation, Brontes' eyes searched mine as if looking for something in them. I faltered, confused and alarmed by his sudden change in demeanor.

"Is that what you think I am?" he grumbled, his voice barely more than a whisper, but the intensity behind it was unmistakable. "A monster?"

"Isn't that what everyone says?" My voice trembled, but I held my ground, staring him down with all the courage I could muster.

He took a step toward me, and I instinctively backed away, suddenly aware of just how close we were. His expression darkened with a blazing fury that sent shivers down my spine.

"Fine!" he growled. "If that is how you truly see me, then there is nothing left to say."

With that, Brontes stormed out of the library with the book clutched tightly in his hand. The door slammed shut behind him, quaking through the walls as if the Storm Castle were trembling in response to his anger.

Frozen in the spot where our confrontation had taken place, the weight of my words settled on me like a thick fog, suffocating any semblance of satisfaction I'd momentarily felt for standing up to the prince. I called him a monster.

Monster.

The word echoed in my mind, and I questioned whether it was justified or if I had allowed anger to cloud my judgment. What had I done? I sank into the nearest chair, my legs suddenly too weak to support me, and clutched its carved arms. My chest felt hollow, echoing with confusion and dismay.

Despite his rage and barbed words, there was still something about him that I couldn't quite put my finger on—something that made me question his fearsome reputation.

Why did his anger evaporate so quickly? And why did seeing that change in his eyes leave me feeling gutted? No matter how many times I replayed the scene over and over in my mind, I didn't understand. I was never meant to understand.

I pressed my fingers to my temples in frustration. If only I were better at reading expressions, at understanding the subtle nuances of body language. But how could I be, when my entire life had been spent learning to suppress my own emotions?

A strong gust of wind rattled against the windows of the library, and the scent of oncoming rain clung to the air. Perhaps it was a reminder of Brontes' turbulent nature. What stormy emotions were swirling inside him now after I called him a monster?

The word slipped from my lips like a dagger. The instant it was out, I knew I'd cut deeper than intended. And yet, I couldn't quite comprehend why it made him so upset. Surely, it wasn't the first time he'd been called that.

Clasping my hands together, I tried to focus on the sensation of my fingers pressing into one another, grounding myself in the present moment. But the look on Brontes' face before he stormed away refused to fade. As the storm clouds above threatened to unleash their fury upon the kingdom, I realized that he was even more of a mystery to me now than he'd ever been. And it would take more than a heated exchange of words to unravel the enigma that was the Storm Prince.

With a groan, I buried my face in my hands. Mother had warned me again and again not to let my emotions show. Now I saw the wisdom in her words. If I hadn't lashed out, if I had kept my feelings contained as I was bred to do, I wouldn't be sitting here now, pulse racing and thoughts in turmoil.

Why did I suddenly feel like the monster?

Start reading *Taken by the Storm Prince* NOW!

Scan below

https://arielrenner.com/tsp

LOVE THIS BOOK?

Want more fantasy & paranormal romance from Ariel Renner? Get a free book when you sign up for her email newsletter.

Get your free book now!

https://arielrenner.com/free-book

ALSO BY ARIEL RENNER

Enchanted Realm Prequel

Fated to the Fire Enemy

Haven Academy

Forbidden Ice Prince
Taken by the Storm Prince
A Storm of Fire and Ice

Standalone Titles

My Fated Protector

For up-to-date information on all of Ariel Renner's titles,
please visit: **arielrenner.com/books**

Printed in Great Britain
by Amazon